PURRFECTLY DOGGED

THE MYSTERIES OF MAX 19

NIC SAINT

PURRFECTLY DOGGED

The Mysteries of Max 19

Copyright © 2020 by Nic Saint

Edited by Chereese Graves

www.nicsaint.com

Give feedback on the book at: info@nicsaint.com

facebook.com/nicsaintauthor
@nicsaintauthor

First Edition

Printed in the U.S.A

*V*ictor Ball was wending his way home on his bicycle after an evening spent at his favorite bar. His bike was swaying across the narrow dirt road, as its owner had had a teensy-weensy too much to drink.

Victor, a middle-aged man with a formidable handlebar mustache and a sizable paunch, was singing loudly and out of key. He was in excellent mood, which was not unusual after imbibing his body weight in alcohol, and if he had trouble navigating the road that led to his modest home, where his wife had presumably given up waiting for him and had retired to bed, he didn't show it.

In fact it was a minor miracle that he managed to stay upright at all, but he did, and with every mighty push on his pedals he was another couple of inches closer to home.

And he would probably have made it, without aiming his rusty old bike into a ditch, if not suddenly a dark figure had loomed up large and menacing while crossing his path.

Victor, even though drunk as a skunk, still had the presence of mind to pull his brakes and stare at the figure. It was not the kind of thing a man in his state of inebriation was accustomed to: the figure wasn't merely large and imposing, it was also possessed of the kind of sharp fangs and glittering red eyes one usually only sees in movies. Its furry hide was shiny and thick, its pointy ears erect, its lips drawn back into a menacing snarl.

If someone had asked him at that moment to describe the hideous creature, he would have told them it was a wolf, and a very strange wolf at that, for the creature was walking on its hind legs, its front paws clawing the air with distinct malice in mind.

And then, as the monster threw its head back and howled at the full moon, Victor finally did what any sane man in his position would have done: he uttered a broken cry of anguish and terror, dropped his bike, and ran off in the opposite direction as fast as his weak-kneed legs would carry him.

The monster, meanwhile, instead of pouncing on this easy prey—this plump and juicy victim—continued howling at that big ball of cheese in the sky, then turned on its mighty heel and vanished into the woods, presumably eager to scare another drunkard.

2

*M*arge Poole was cleaning her attic. She'd long wanted to take a broom and a duster to the cluttered space and get rid of some of the stuff that had been piling up there for years, but had never found the time—or the willpower. But when she'd been up there the week before and had almost been crushed by a falling stack of books, she'd decided to tackle the matter head-on. So she'd changed into a set of old clothes, had tied a scarf around her head, and had mounted those stairs with a take-no-prisoners attitude.

And she'd just gone through the first rickety rack, when she'd come upon an old photo album and had been idly leafing through it with a wistful expression on her face.

The pictures in the album were of her and her first boyfriend Jock Farnsworth. She'd known Jock long before she'd ever met her current husband Tex, and seeing those old photos of her and Jock brought back a lot of memories.

And she'd been sitting there reminiscing, having forgotten all about attics that needed to be cleaned out, when a voice suddenly sounded from downstairs.

"Mom! Are you up there? Mom?"

"Up here, honey!" she shouted.

Her daughter Odelia's head came peeping up through the attic door, a quizzical look on her face. "What are you doing?" she asked, glancing around at the cluttered space. "Yikes. Someone needs to clean this mess up."

"Well, I was, actually," said Marge, "but then I came upon this album full of old pictures and I kind of lost track of time."

Odelia joined her and took the album. "Is that you? You look so young!"

"I do, don't I? I was even younger than you are in these pictures. Sixteen, seventeen."

"And who's that guy with you?"

"Jock Farnsworth. We were boyfriend and girlfriend two summers long, until he broke it off and hooked up with Grace Beasley instead." She still felt the sting of betrayal at the memory, even though she'd hardly thought about Jock or Grace for years.

"Jock Farnsworth, as in chicken wing king Jock Farnsworth?"

"Didn't I tell you about him? I thought I did. Or maybe I didn't. Yes, Jock and I were together for a while, until we weren't. But then I met your dad and so all's well that ends well. If I'd stayed with Jock I'd never have met Tex, so it was all for the best—even though I didn't see it that way at the time."

"Imagine that," said Odelia as she leafed through the album. "The richest man in Hampton Cove could have been my dad."

Marge laughed. "Yeah, I guess he could have been."

"Are they still together, Jock and this Grace person?"

"Last time I heard they were."

"I think I've seen his daughter at the office once. She's Dan's goddaughter."

"Oh, that's right. Isn't Jock one of the *Gazette*'s main sponsors?"

"He is. Dan owes a great deal to the Farnsworth chicken wing bling."

"Well, it's all ancient history to me," said Marge, closing the photo album and coughing at the cloud of dust this stirred up. "Want to help me clean up?"

"I can't. I have a meeting with Dan. He told me to come down to the office pronto."

"Did something happen?"

"No idea. Usually when it does he tells me over the phone."

"Better get going then. You know Dan doesn't like to be kept waiting."

"Are you sure you'll be able to handle this, Mom? If you keep going down memory lane, you'll never get this finished."

"Oh, I'll be fine," said Marge. "I'll ask your dad to give me a hand when he gets home."

Odelia descended the creaky stairs and Marge put the photo album in a box with stuff she intended to keep, then took a deep breath and tackled the attic with renewed fervor, this time vowing not to let the ghosts of her dead past snag her attention again.

The Jock episode was ancient history. She'd long ago forgiven him for dumping her for Grace and she now decided not to devote another minute of her time to the man.

❧

"Slow down, Victor," said Chase. "You're not making any sense."

Chief Alec had walked into the interview room and took a seat on the edge of the table. "Still drunk, huh? I thought a night in the drunk tank would have sobered you up."

"I'm not drunk, Chief!" said Victor. "I'm stone-cold sober!" His eyes were wide and red-rimmed, and his large mustache was trembling.

"He's drunk," said Chase. "He just told me the same story he told the desk sergeant last night."

"About the werewolf?" Alec grunted.

"It *was* a werewolf, I swear!" said Victor. "I saw it as clearly as I'm seeing you! He was standing not ten feet away from me, growling and howling and he had these claws, at least three inches long, and his teeth were glittering and dripping with saliva!"

"Yeah, yeah, yeah," said Alec. "I think it's time for you to head on home, buddy."

"But I really saw it! It was going to attack me but I was too quick. I ran and ran and I came straight here—but when I told them what happened they didn't believe me!"

"I know you came straight here, and my desk sergeant put you straight into the lockup, as you were drunk out of your skull, Victor."

"I had a few too many to drink, that's true," Victor allowed, "but as soon as I saw that monster I sobered up. I swear I'm telling you the truth, Chief. You have to believe me."

Chief Alec exchanged a look of understanding with his deputy, and Chase got up. "Let's get you out of here," he told Victor.

"But… aren't you going to finish taking my statement? People need to be warned. You need to call in the army—the National Guard—the FBI!"

"We'll call in Mulder and Scully," said Chase, as he clasped a heavy hand on the man's shoulder. "And you can tell them all about your encounter with that nasty werewolf."

"And while I talk to this Mully Sculder, you'll hunt that beast down, won't you?"

"Oh, of course we will, Victor," said the Chief with a grin. "We'll go after that thing with everything we've got—don't you worry. This is now my number one priority."

"When the reporters show up, tell them I saw it first, will you? And make sure they spell my name right. That's Victor with a C. And Ball with a B."

"Let's go, Victor with a C," said Chase, and led the man out of the room.

"What a nut," Alec muttered.

"Just look at it, Max, Just take a good, close look."

I didn't have to take a good, close look. Even from a distance I knew what it was: dog poo.

"It's a disgrace," said Shanille. "An absolute disgrace."

"You're not wrong," I said.

Even though Shanille had come to us with the problem, depositing it in our laps, so to speak, she wasn't the first one to have noticed an issue that was troubling the entire feline community.

Dog poo was a problem that had long irked me, and I'd mentioned it to Odelia many, many times.

"You have to talk to your human," Shanille said now. "She has to write an article about this. These dogs are defacing our beautiful town—they're turning Hampton Cove into the garbage dump of the Hamptons. If this keeps up no tourist will want to visit our beautiful town and then where will we be? In the scrapheap of history! The doldrums!"

"It would be very peaceful," said Dooley, who didn't seem to grasp the big picture.

"I think Shanille is right," said Harriet. "Dog poo is the

biggest issue of our time. A major menace to public health and safety. Something we desperately need to address."

"It's pretty nasty," Brutus agreed.

The five of us were standing around what could very well be the largest dog turd I'd ever come across in my long and illustrious career as a cat sleuth. And I didn't even need to take a sniff to know whom it belonged to either: Marge and Tex's neighbors had recently gotten a dog, and I had every reason to believe this turd belonged to that dog.

"People step in it," Shanille pointed out as a man carefully sidestepped the pile of steaming dog dung and shook his head in annoyance. "Cats step in it. We all step in it."

"I don't step in it," I pointed out.

"I step in it," said Dooley.

"We *all* step in it," Shanille insisted.

"Eww," Harriet said as she visibly cringed.

"And then they drag that poo into their homes, and it gets smushed into their carpets and smeared across their nice hardwood floors. It gets dragged into nurseries and kitchens. It ends up in bathrooms and bedrooms. It's hideous, it's gross and it needs to be stopped. I know, for Father Reilly curses about the horrible muck every single day."

"Father Reilly curses?" asked Dooley. "I thought priests weren't supposed to curse?"

"He uses colorful language, but never takes the Lord's name in vain," said Shanille prissily.

Father Reilly is Shanille's human, and runs one of the biggest churches in Hampton Cove. And since many people set foot in that church, I could only imagine the amounts of dog poo they trailed inside.

"Just think about it for a moment," she said now. "Let's take as a very conservative estimate that one out of ten people step in dog poo, and that all of those people drag that poo into my church. That's a lot of dog poo to clean up for poor Father Reilly."

"I'm sure Father Reilly doesn't clean his church himself, though, right?" I said.

"No, he has a cleaning lady, but the principle still stands: someone has to clean up the poo. And why? Simply because dog owners refuse to clean up after their dogs. If you want a dog, you should accept the responsibility and remove the poo," said Shanille with the kind of forcefulness that has served her well as director of cat choir. I mean, if you can wrangle the entire Hampton Cove cat community, you can wrangle anything.

"I don't think it's the owners that should take the responsibility, though," said Harriet, who hates dog poo even more than the rest of us. Her gorgeous white fur is more susceptible to being sullied and soiled than mine or Dooley's or Brutus's.

"You don't?" said Shanille.

"Of course not. Just look at us cats. We do our business nicely and hygienically in a litter box, which is conveniently scented so as not to let the foul stench upset sensitive noses. Afterward, we clean our tushies all by ourselves. Compare that to dogs. Do they use litter boxes? No, they simply pee against trees and poo on the sidewalk. Yuck! And then, to make matters worse, they don't even clean themselves! Double yuck! So you can see how the responsibility of this dog poo crisis lies with the dogs, not humans."

"I think it might be a shared responsibility," said Brutus.

"No, sweetie pie, if we do our doo next to the litter box, is it Odelia's fault, or Marge or Gran's? No, it's our mistake, and we should be the ones suffering the consequences. But if a dog does his business on the floor, nobody cares! And that's the big issue here."

"So what do you suggest?" asked Shanille.

"I suggest we immediately start a campaign to teach dogs to use a litter box, just like cats. I mean, how hard can it be? If we can do it, dogs can do it, too, right?"

"But dogs aren't as smart as cats," said Dooley. "Are they, Max?"

"No, obviously they're not," I said. "Otherwise they would have learned how to go on the potty a long time ago."

"Human babies learn to go on the potty when they're two or three," said Harriet, "so why can't we teach dogs to do the same? It would save us the agony of having to look at that." She wrinkled her nose as she gestured at the big pile of doo, stinking up the street.

"It's a disgrace," Shanille repeated her earlier estimation. "But I don't know if dogs are even capable of being potty-trained. I mean, like you said, dogs are pretty dumb."

"Yes, but surely they're not as dumb as that," said Harriet.

"This is a historic day," said Shanille, who, as a priest's cat, possesses the gift of the gab. "This is the day when five cats decided not to take it any longer. When five cats took a stand and said, enough is enough! No more! We are going to tackle an issue that has plagued our community for far too long." Her face had taken on an appropriately earnest expression. "We, ladies and gentlecats, are going to potty-train dogs."

"Yes, we are," said Harriet, sounding cautiously pleased.

"And may the world never be the same again," Shanille added.

"Amen," I said. Shanille always has that effect on me.

---

4

*O*delia, after her short detour to her mother's attic, finally arrived at *Gazette* headquarters. She made a beeline for her editor's office and when she burst in, saw that he wasn't alone. A pretty young woman with auburn tresses and refined features sat across from him, looking teary-faced and visibly upset.

"Oh, finally," said the young lady when Odelia entered. "You have to help me, Miss Poole. You have to help me find my mother!"

Odelia blinked. "Um…" She directed a questioning glance at Dan, but the white-bearded editor simply stared back at her, a grim expression on his face.

When he finally spoke, there was a catch in his voice. "I don't believe you've met my goddaughter, Odelia. This is Alicia. Alicia, you know Odelia. My finest reporter."

Odelia would have mentioned she was also Dan's only reporter, but the moment didn't seem to lend itself to levity. Instead, she shook the young woman's hand and took a seat. "Such a strange coincidence. I was just talking about your dad with my mother."

"Marge Poole. She works at the library, doesn't she? She's nice. Very sweet and kind."

"She is," Odelia confirmed.

"Alicia is Jock and Grace Farnsworth's daughter," said Dan. "Her mother has gone missing, and I want you to drop everything and help find her, Odelia. I don't care what you're working on—this is now your number one priority, you understand?"

Odelia didn't understand a thing. "But if your mother has disappeared, shouldn't you go to the police? They're more equipped to deal with missing persons cases than I am."

"I can't go to the police. My father would kill me. He's probably going to be extremely upset that I came here to talk to Uncle Dan, but I simply can't stand it anymore."

"Your father doesn't want to involve the police? But why?"

"He thinks Mama didn't disappear. He thinks she ran away... with her boyfriend."

"Your mother has a boyfriend?"

Alicia nodded. "He's an artist," she said, as if that explained everything.

"And... you don't believe they ran away together?"

"Mama would never leave without telling me. We're very close—we're more best friends than mother and daughter. She wouldn't simply up and leave and not let me know. She simply wouldn't."

She'd pressed a tissue to her nose while tears still rolled across her cheeks.

"Look, it's not because your father doesn't want to involve the police that you can't," said Odelia. "She's your mother, and if you have reason to believe her disappearance is troubling, you should tell my uncle. If you want I'll come with you. Chief Alec is a very nice man and very capable. He'll find your mother."

13

"My father would never speak to me again. He thinks it's bad enough the servants know, and now to involve the police…" She shook her head. "No way. Besides, what if he's right? What if Mama simply ran away with her lover? The police aren't going to be able to bring her back. She's a grown woman. She'll simply refuse to come with them."

"See what I mean?" said Dan, who was clearly worried about his godchild. "You have to find Grace, Odelia. And if you're worried about expenses, don't be. I'll pay you out of my own pocket to find her."

"And I'll pay you the rest," said Alicia. "I just want to know what happened to her. If she did run away, that's her business. I just want to know, so that I can stop worrying."

"Do you know the name of this artist boyfriend?" asked Odelia, taking out her notebook and pencil.

"His name is Fabio Shakespeare. He's a painter and he lives in a small cottage on our domain. Papa wanted to kick him out when he first started suspecting he was having an affair with Mama, but Mama convinced him not to. My parents have been living separate lives for years. They live in different wings of the house, so it's not as if Mama was really doing anything wrong when she got involved with Fabio."

"What do you know about this Fabio?"

"Oh, he's wonderful. A real genius. You should see his paintings. He painted my portrait, too, and it's the most amazing thing."

She clearly seemed taken with this painter, Odelia thought. "So you didn't mind that your mother was having an affair with him?"

"No, I was happy for her. Very happy. Papa is… a difficult man to live with. Even I find him hard to tolerate. I mean, don't get me wrong, I love my father, but he's very tough and demanding—not sweet and loving, like Fabio, and definitely not a romantic."

Odelia nodded. "Do you think your dad will mind if I ask him a couple of questions and snoop around?"

"No, I think it's fine, as long as you promise not to tell anyone."

"Be discreet," said Dan. "Be very discreet, Odelia. And Alicia, tell your dad I'm not going to print anything about this. This is not newspaper business to me—this is personal."

"Oh, thank you so much, Uncle Dan," said Alicia, as she rounded the desk and gave her godfather a big hug. "I won't forget this."

"It's the least I can do for my precious goddaughter," said Dan warmly.

"So when did your mother disappear, exactly?" asked Odelia.

"Um… the last time I saw her was the day before yesterday. At breakfast. We were supposed to head into town that afternoon to do some shopping, but she never showed up. And then the next day when I checked her room I saw that her bed hadn't been slept in. I decided to tell Papa, who hadn't even noticed Mama had gone missing, and he told me to wait another day, just to be sure. And so this morning, when I told him Mama was still nowhere to be found, he told me in no uncertain terms I shouldn't get the police involved, and that Mama had probably eloped with Fabio."

"Did you check to see if Fabio is gone, too?"

"I did. Immediately. And he's gone. Packed his bags and disappeared."

"So that would suggest your father is right."

"I guess so, but like I said, Mama would never leave without telling me. She simply wouldn't."

"Have you tried calling her?"

"Of course. I've called and texted—but she's not picking up and not responding to my texts. Oh, Miss Poole, you have to find her. I'm so scared something bad has happened."

"I will find her, Alicia," she said, even as she wondered if she was making a promise she wouldn't be able to keep. "Trust me."

5

*G*ran walked out of the house and closed the door behind her. As she passed us, presumably on her way to the office, she paused. "What's going on here? Are you guys having a meeting?"

"Yes, we are," said Dooley promptly. "We've just formed the first-ever Cat Committee for the Re-education of Canines, also known as the CCREC."

"Crack? What crack?" asked Gran. "I don't see no crack."

"We want to teach dogs not to poo in the street," Harriet explained.

"Yes, we want to re-educate dogs. Make them more like cats," Shanille added.

Gran guffawed. "Good luck with that!"

"But, Gran, just look at it. Isn't it a disgrace?" said Harriet, gesturing to the still steaming pile of dog dung.

Gran looked at the evidence of a dog's bowel movement and frowned. "Who left that there?"

"I think it belongs to Rufus," said Harriet. "Marcie and Ted's new dog?"

"Not on my watch!" said Gran, and immediately stalked

over to Marcie's doorstep and mashed the bell with her finger.

"Your Grandma Muffin could be a most formidable ally," said Shanille.

We watched on as the door opened and Marcie appeared. She's a dark-haired slender woman of Marge's age, and very sweet. "Oh, hey, Vesta," she said. "So nice to see you."

"What were you thinking, Marcie?" said Gran, shaking her head. "What were you thinking when you left that stinking heap of stinky doo stinking up my sidewalk?!" She pointed an accusatory finger at the turd.

Marcie looked past Gran and frowned. "That's not mine."

"I know it's not yours. It's your dog's."

"Impossible," said Marcie. "Ted always picks up after Rufus. He would never leave our baby's doo-doo just lying around for people to step in. No way. Nuh-uh."

"My cats think it's Rufus's, and my cats are never wrong," said Gran, and too late realized her faux-pas.

"How would you know what your cats think?" asked Marcie with a laugh. "Unless the rumors are true, and you Poole girls really can talk to your cats."

"Never mind," Gran grumbled, and executed a strategic retreat. "I shouldn't have said that," she muttered when she'd joined us on the sidewalk again. "Now Marcie will blab about it everywhere she goes. That's the way she operates." She stared at the heap of poo. "How sure are you that this belongs to Marcie's dog, on a scale of one to ten?"

"Ten," said Harriet immediately. "All excrement has a particular scent, and I needed only one sniff to know this particular pile belongs to Rufus."

"Mh." Gran directed a not-so-friendly look at Marcie's house, where presumably Marcie was at that moment watching us from behind her curtains. "You know what? You cats just gave me a fantastic idea. A real scorcher."

18

And without further explanation, she took off and left.

"So now what?" asked Brutus.

"Now we start our re-education campaign," said Harriet. "And we begin with the culprit of this here eyesore."

"You're not serious," said Brutus. "You're going to try and re-educate Rufus?"

"Yes, I am," said Harriet, "and so are you."

"Ugh," said Brutus, and I like to think that he spoke for all of us.

I mean, it's one thing to engage in idle talk about the re-education of dogs and teaching them how to be potty-trained, but another to actually go out and do it. Dogs, you see, don't take kindly to interference from cats, and Rufus is a big dog. A sheepdog. Those big and woolly ones? Some-times I think there must have been a woolly mammoth among his forebears. I hadn't really made Rufus's acquain-tance, apart from the occasional greeting across the fence, but if there is one thing a long life lived in Hampton Cove has taught me, it is always to steer clear of dogs, especially the really big ones.

We don't bother them, and they don't bother us. Peaceful coexistence if you will.

But Harriet was already on her way over, and so we followed. We couldn't very well backtrack now, even though Shanille herself had suddenly turned a little thoughtful at this denouement.

"Are you sure this is a good idea, Max?" she asked as we stepped into Marge and Tex's backyard.

"I think it's a terrible idea," I said, not mincing my words. "But you know what's an even worse idea? To try and stop Harriet once her mind is made up about something."

"Yeah, I know," said Shanille. "Remember I tried to take away her solo spot on the choir? She hasn't stopped bugging me about it since. I'm starting to think I could have saved myself a lot of trouble if I'd simply let her keep it."

"That's generally the best way to deal with Harriet," I agreed.

"Hey, you guys," said Dooley, "do you realize that CCREC sounds like CRACK? Isn't that funny?"

"Very funny, Dooley," I said.

"Because we're going to teach dogs to clean their—"

"Let's keep it civil, Dooley," said Shanille reproachfully.

"I was going to say back," said Dooley. "As in backside?"

"Oh, that's all right then."

"Thanks, Shanille, and can I just say I think it's wonderful what you're trying to do? I stepped in dog doo just the other day and I didn't like it. It was soft and squishy at first, but then it was stinky and horrible the next. Max had to help me clean it off, and it took a long time and it involved sticking my paw in a puddle of water, and it wasn't a lot of fun."

"It happened to me, too, Dooley," said Shanille, "so I can definitely relate."

"And then when it didn't come off, we had to tell Odelia, and she decided to give me a bath and I hate taking a bath, don't you? Water is so wet!"

"Water generally is very wet," Shanille agreed.

"The dog doo had gotten stuck between my claws and my little pink pads, and Odelia had to use tissues and even a toothbrush at some point, and it tickled!"

"I can only imagine," Shanille muttered.

"And then she had to throw away the toothbrush because she said she couldn't use it anymore after she'd used it on me to clean away all of that dog excrement—I love that word dog excrement, don't you, Shanille? Dog excrement. It's such a funny word. I didn't understand what she meant at first, but now I do. Dog excrement. So funny."

"Oh, Dooley," Shanille groaned, and I think she already regretted dropping by.

We'd finally reached the fence that divides Tex and Marge's backyard from Marcie and Ted's, and Harriet loudly said, "Rufus, oh, Rufus, where art thou?"

Unfortunately there is no hole in the fence, but there is a nice garden table on which us cats can jump to have a good overview of the backyard next door, so we did so now.

Rufus, who'd come lumbering up, directed a curious glance in our direction. He didn't need a table to step on, as he can easily look across the fence. Yes, he's that big. "Oh, hey, Harriet—hey, guys. So nice to see you. How are you?"

"Rufus, we need to talk," said Harriet, adopting her best re-educational voice.

"Oh, sure, Harriet," said Rufus. "Anytime. Oh, hey, Shanille. Haven't seen you around in a while. Everything all right? Father Reilly doing okay? Good. That's great to hear."

"He's very nice," said Dooley.

"Yes, he is very nice," I agreed. Rufus is probably one of the nicest dogs we know.

"So the thing is, Rufus," said Harriet, deciding not to get sidetracked by all this waffle from the peanut gallery, "that you left a horrible mess on the sidewalk just now."

"I did? I wasn't aware—I'm so sorry, Harriet. I'm truly very, very sorry."

"Apology accepted, but that doesn't change the fact that people are going to step in the product of your defecation. So here's my suggestion. Why don't you learn to go on the potty? It's clean, it's pleasant, and it's a much better solution for everyone involved."

"The... potty? What do you mean, Harriet? What is this potty you're talking about?"

"Well, I don't know if you're familiar with the concept of the litter box?"

"I think I've heard about it, but I've never actually seen one," said Rufus.

"Max. Please explain to Rufus what a litter box is," said Harriet.

I stared at her. I'd had no idea she'd penciled me in for a starring role in this little pantomime of hers.

"Well, go on, then. Tell him."

I cleared my throat. "A litter box is literally a box filled with litter, Rufus. You, um, do your business inside the box, and the litter absorbs all the annoying odors and whatnot. And then when it comes time to clean out the box, all your humans have to do is scoop out the affected litter, deposit it in a little plastic bag—or, in your case, a very large plastic bag —and put it out on trash day for garbage collection."

"Easy-peasy, and so much fun!" said Harriet.

"It does sound like fun," Rufus agreed. "And where can I find these litter boxes?"

"Um… I guess you'll have to discuss that with your human," said Harriet. "For your size and shape I'd advise the extra-large model. Possibly the extra extra extra large."

"I'm not sure they have litter boxes for a dog of Rufus's size," I told Harriet.

"I'm not so sure either," said Shanille, as she took in the voluminous mass of dog.

"Doesn't matter," said Harriet. "If people want litter boxes in Rufus's size, the companies producing litter boxes will produce them. It is simply a matter of supply and demand. Now scoot and don't forget to tell your human, Rufus."

"Um… there's only one problem with that," said Rufus.

"Oh? And what's that?"

"I can't talk to my human."

"Mh…" I could tell that Harriet was stumped for a moment. She turned to us and said, "Ad hoc meeting of the

CCREC. How do we get dogs to tell their humans to buy them a litter box?"

It was a tough one, and for a moment we were all stumped, then suddenly Dooley said, "We could ask Gran to join the CCREC. And then she can tell the dog owners."

"Excellent idea, Dooley!" said Harriet, and turned back to Rufus, who still stood eyeing us with a kindly expression on his furry face. "For now, try to familiarize yourself with the concept of the litter box, Rufus."

"Like an Olympian," said Dooley.

"Tell him, Dooley," said Harriet encouragingly. "Tell Rufus how it is."

"Well," said Dooley, "Olympians visualize their victories. So you have to visualize stepping into the litter box, being inside the litter box, doing your business in the litter box… basically *being* the litter box."

"Being the litter box," said Rufus, nodding. "Gotcha."

Harriet beamed and patted Dooley on the head, not unlike a circus director whose monkey has just performed a complicated trick.

---

6

*A*s Chase made his way to the copy machine, he noticed to his surprise how Dolores was seated behind one of the desks in the main office, going through a stack of files. He approached the desk sergeant. "Dolores? What are you doing? Shouldn't you be behind your desk?"

"The Mayor told me to go and sit here," she said in her typical smoker's rasp. Her mascara was prominently applied, as usual, making her more than a little scary-looking.

"The Mayor? What do you mean?"

"He came by earlier and told me to sit here. When I asked him what I was supposed to do, he said to figure something out to keep me busy until he could arrange for my early retirement, so I just thought I'd do some filing. There's always filing to be done."

"But… if you're here, who's sitting at your desk?"

"Fiona," she said acerbically.

Chase's face darkened. "The Mayor's niece?"

Dolores nodded. "She took my place. The Mayor said the precinct needed some livening up. Said he had received lots of complaints about me. About how my grumpy old mug scares people away."

"He said that, did he?"

"Yes, he did. And then he told Fiona to take a seat and look pretty and he left."

"Don't go anywhere," said Chase.

"Oh, I'm not going anywhere."

"I'll fix this."

"Good luck with that," she growled without much enthusiasm.

Chase stalked down the corridor and burst into the Chief's office. "Did you know the Mayor just told Dolores to take a seat in the main office and put his niece in her place?"

"Yeah, he told me," said the Chief, not looking happy.

"But he can't do that!"

"He can. He's the mayor."

"And you're chief of police. Just tell him he can't just kick out Dolores!"

"He can and he did. And he also told me that if I make a fuss, he's sure he'll be able to find himself a new chief of police, too."

Chase had planted his hands on the Chief's desk and stared at the man. "He said that?"

"He did, and what's worse—he means it. Ever since we played hooky at that conference he's got it in for us, Chase. It wouldn't surprise me if he decided to kick me to the curb. And as for you, it's a miracle he hasn't put you in charge of policing traffic on Bay Avenue yet."

"He wouldn't do that."

"Oh, he would. He hates my guts, and now he hates your guts, too. It's all falling apart, Chase. Thirty years on the job, and it's all going to pieces. Soon I'll be forced out, and you'll be telling road ragers to please calm down."

There was a knock on the door, and Officer Sarah Flunk stuck her head in. "Chief, Victor Ball says he wants a word."

"Victor is still here? I thought you sent him on his merry way?"

"I did," said Chase.

"Um… he says he's afraid to go home," said Sarah. "In case he runs into the big monster again. What is he talking about, Chief?"

"Never mind what he's talking about," said the Chief with a touch of pique. "Just send him home and tell him not to bother us again with his nonsense."

"Will do, Chief," said the officer, and retracted her head and closed the door.

"We can't just let the Mayor take over," said Chase. "Dolores has done that job for ages—probably since Hampton Cove was incorporated—and a damn fine job she's done, too."

"And so she has, but what do you want me to do? My hands are tied here, Chase."

"Maybe we shouldn't have flunked out of that conference," Chase said now, plunking himself down on a seat.

They'd both recently gone to LA for a police conference, but the subject matter hadn't appealed neither to Chase or Chief Alec, so they'd decided to play truant. Their absence had been duly noted, and the Mayor had been notified, and he hadn't liked it. Possibly because the town had paid for the hotel and expenses.

"Oh, I'm pretty sure this conference business is just an excuse," said the Chief. "He's been wanting to put his niece in Dolores's spot for weeks. Next stop: this desk," he said, patting his own desk.

It was no secret the Mayor had big plans for his favorite niece. Preferably he'd like to see her run the police station as its first woman chief. And this was only the first step.

The door flew open again, and Victor Ball walked in, his mustache bristling. "You can't send me home, Chief! That monster will be waiting for me, I just know it will!"

"If it was, don't you think your wife would have called by now?" said the Chief.

"Alice! That thing will have eaten her alive! Oh, you have to send a squad car to take me home. Alice might still be alive if we hurry."

"Oh, go on home, Victor."

"But, Chief!"

"Go! Now!"

And Victor went, though without much conviction.

"I'll talk to the Mayor," said Chase. "I'll tell him this is no way to treat a loyal police officer like Dolores."

"Are you sure? He might decide to kick you off the force right then and there."

"Let him try."

The door flew open again, and this time the Chief's mother burst in.

"I just had the best idea ever!" she announced.

"Ma, can't you see I'm in a meeting?"

She ignored him and sat down next to Chase. "You're going to start fining people who let their dogs do their business on the sidewalk. Step one. Then you're going to announce your candidacy for mayor. Step two. And finally, once you're mayor of this fine town of ours, you're going to start campaigning for governor. And then, finally, for president! And I'll be there every step of the way, don't you worry, son. I'll be your campaign manager. I know exactly how it works. I've seen it on TV."

"Ma, how many times do I have to tell you? I don't want to be mayor. I like being chief. And tell me something, how is fining dog owners going to help me become mayor?"

"Simple math! Thirty percent of the people in this town are cat owners, right?"

"If you say so."

"Thirty percent are dog owners, and thirty percent got no pets. That means sixty percent of the people have to suffer because thirty percent refuse to pick up after their dogs. So if you go after the dog people hard, those other sixty percent are gonna be so grateful they're gonna vote you into town hall. See? Math!"

"You left out ten percent of the population," said Chase.

"Oh, don't let's split hairs," said Vesta.

"Not so simple, Ma," said Alec. "First off, like Chase already indicated, I'm not so sure about your numbers, and second, most people clean up after their dogs. It's only a very small minority that doesn't. And to go after those people all heavy-handed is not the way I like to do things as chief. You know that."

"Well, you should. People love the Dirty Harry approach, not that namby-pamby community policing business. They want you to go in hard. Bust some heads and rattle some cages. You need to arrest those jaypoopers and you'll be mayor in no time!"

"I'm not going to arrest people for not picking up after their dogs, Ma."

"Look, you're going to run for mayor and I'm going to be your campaign manager. And don't argue with me, Alec Lip! I'm your mother and a mother knows!" And with these words she stalked out again, leaving the Chief to bang his head against the desk.

"What did I ever do to deserve this, Chase? What?!"

"I'm sure she doesn't mean it, Chief."

"Oh, yes, she does. Her campaign has already begun, and with the Mayor gunning for me, this is not going to improve my chances of staying in this chair for much longer."

"Don't worry, Chief. I'll talk to the Mayor and you talk to your mother. We'll fix this."

But the Chief was not to be consoled.

7

*M*arge walked into the library feeling like she'd forgotten something. And as she entered and closed the door behind her, she suddenly heard a loud banging sound. She smiled and headed to the staircase that led into the basement. Someone was working hard.

There were racks and racks of books and old files in the basement, and the banging sounds continued as she made her way in their direction. And then, as she reached the back wall, she suddenly remembered what it was she'd forgotten.

"Oh, you guys, I'm so sorry but I completely forgot," she said as she addressed the two men hard at work there.

They both looked up, startled. Johnny Carew and Jerry Vale were two ex-convicts who'd recently been granted a lighter sentence. Instead of spending the remainder of their time inside, they'd been allowed to do community service instead.

So Marge had magnanimously agreed when their probation officer had asked if there was any chance they'd be able to work at the library to fulfill the terms of their service.

She wanted to have the basement redone, starting with

the back wall, which was suffering from an acute case of mold and rot and needed to be torn out and rebuilt.

"I said I'd bake you a cake and I completely forgot," she said.

"Oh, that's all right, Mrs. P," said Jerry, a smallish man with a face like a ferret.

"No cake?" asked Johnny, his partner in crime. He was a very large man with a perpetually dumb look on his large, square mug.

"I'll bake you one tonight," said Marge. "I promise. I had this sudden urge to clean out the attic this morning, and totally forgot about your cake."

"Don't sweat it, Mrs. P," said Jerry. "Tomorrow is fine."

She studied the wall with interest. "And? Have you discovered the source of that rot?"

"Nah, not yet," said Jerry, who looked a little jumpy, Marge thought. "But we're getting there, isn't that right, Johnny?"

"Oh, sure, we're getting there, Mrs. P," said Johnny.

"Marge, please," she said.

"Probably a neighbor with a leak in his bathroom," said Jerry.

"Yeah, probably a leak," said Johnny.

"Or bad plumbing."

"Yeah, bad plumbing," Johnny echoed.

"Well, I'll leave you boys to it," she said. "Yell if you need anything, all right?"

"Will do, Mrs. P—Marge," said Jerry.

"No cake, Jerry," she heard Johnny tell his friend as she started walking away. "I was really looking forward to that cake."

"Oh, shut up, you moron. How many times do I have to tell you? You talk too much."

"But, Jerry!"

"You talk too much!"

"But I like cake!"

"Shut up!"

And as she mounted the stairs, she told herself not to forget about that cake this time. Johnny obviously had been looking forward to it. He and Jerry might be criminals, but they were clearly well on the road to rehabilitation, and she'd decided she would do her bit to help them become upstanding citizens once more.

The two men had actually broken into Odelia's house not so long ago, and had been caught red-handed by Odelia's cats. But Marge believed in letting bygones be bygones, and in the power of forgiveness. So it was with a warm heart that she'd welcomed the two former crooks into her library.

And as the clanging and the banging resumed, she soon forgot about the basement, and her thoughts returned to Jock Farnsworth, and Jock's wife Grace. It had been, what, thirty years now? And for no particular reason she found herself wondering how Jock was doing, and Grace. She knew they had a daughter, and she thought the girl would be twenty now. And as she found her mind incapable of staying away from the topic of her ex-boyfriend and his family, suddenly her own daughter walked in, looking solemn.

"Odelia? What's wrong, honey?" she asked.

"Do you remember we were talking about Jock and Grace Farnsworth this morning?"

"What a coincidence! I was just thinking about them!"

"Well, Alicia Farnsworth dropped by the office just now. She thinks something happened to her mother and wants me to investigate."

"Something happened to Grace? What do you mean?"

"She's gone—disappeared. Jock claims she left with her boyfriend, who's also disappeared, but Alicia claims her mother would never go off without telling her, and she has a feeling something must have happened to her. Something bad."

"Oh, my God!"

"Yeah. Could you do me a big favor, Mom, and introduce me to Jock? Maybe smooth the path a little? He won't be happy when he learns his daughter went behind his back and asked me to investigate his wife's disappearance."

Marge hesitated. "I'm not sure if that's such a good idea, honey. Jock and I… it's been a long time, and we didn't exactly part in an amicable way."

"But like you said, it's been a long time, and you have spoken to him since, right?"

"No, I haven't, not really. Oh, sure, I've seen him and Grace in town, but we've never spoken. He broke my heart, Odelia, and I was really upset for a very long time. I thought he was the one, you know, and then he met Grace and it turned out I wasn't the one for him. Grace was."

"Not anymore she's not."

"You say she was having an affair?"

"Yeah, with an artist who lives in a cottage on the domain. Guy called Fabio Shakespeare."

"I think I've heard of him. Specializes in portraits?"

"Specializes in seducing rich married women, apparently."

Marge thought for a moment, then decided that maybe this was a good opportunity to finally leave the past behind. And patch things up with Jock once and for all.

"You're right," she said. "It was a long time ago. And maybe it's time to finally forgive and forget. When do you want to do this?"

"How about now? Can you close up the library for a couple of hours?"

"I could, but I've got an even better idea."

8

"We need recruits," said Harriet, who'd now really and truly taken command of our new association. "We need every cat in Hampton Cove to educate every dog. It's the only way. Otherwise this is going to take forever."

"You know, you and I haven't always seen eye to eye on everything," said Shanille, "but I have to admit you've really taken this dog doo business well in paw, Harriet."

"I think it's important, Shanille. I think this may very well be the most important issue of our time. It touches on so many aspects of our lives: hygiene, discipline, respect for our fellow cats… If we can't fix this, we need to ask ourselves who we are as a nation, you know?"

"She's taking this really serious, isn't she?" asked Brutus, a note of worry in his voice.

I understood where he was coming from. Harriet has a tendency to get carried away with any project she takes on, and this was one project she was digging her teeth into.

"If she keeps this up she's going to antagonize every last

dog in town," Brutus said, "and then the streets won't be safe for us to walk on."

It was an aspect of the matter I hadn't considered. There exists a very fragile peace between cats and dogs. The kind of peace that can be torn apart by a rash act like trying to coerce every dog into adopting the feline way of disposing of their doggie doo.

"Rufus took it pretty well," I said.

"Rufus is a nice dog," said Brutus. "A sweet mutt. But not all dogs are like Rufus, and if Harriet starts ruffling feathers, there's no telling what might happen."

"Don't you mean ruffling dog hairs?" asked Dooley.

Brutus decided to ignore Dooley's contribution. "Dogs may revolt. Turn on us en masse," he said, painting an apocalyptic picture of a war between cats and dogs.

"Maybe you should tell Harriet to take it easy?" I suggested.

"Have you ever tried to tell Harriet anything? She isn't one for taking things easy. She's a can-do cat who doesn't believe in taking prisoners." He sighed. "Let's just see what happens. Maybe Gran will be able to talk some sense into her."

"I don't know…" I said. Asking Gran to talk sense into someone is probably like asking a pyromaniac to put out a fire.

We'd arrived at the doctor's office and now stepped inside. As I had suspected, Gran was seated behind her desk, but instead of playing Solitaire on her computer, like she usually does, she was busily typing away, twin red splotches on her cheekbones a testament to her excitement.

"Hey, Gran," said Harriet as we walked behind the desk.

"Hey, you," she said without looking up or taking a break from typing.

"We have a proposition for you," said Harriet, not deterred by Gran's obvious lack of interest in our presence. "We want you to join our newly formed association."

"We want you to become a CCREC'er," said Dooley proudly.

"Did you just call me a cracker?" said Gran, and finally stopped typing.

"Well, only if you want to," said Dooley, slightly taken aback by her hard stare.

"Watch your tongue, young feline," said Gran, wagging a menacing forefinger.

"Hear us out first," said Shanille, deciding to intervene before things got ugly.

"Shanille? Shouldn't you be helping Father Reilly convert a few more souls?" said Gran, who hasn't been Father Reilly's biggest fan ever since he told her that her soul would probably go to hell for cursing so much.

"Just listen to Shanille, Gran," said Harriet. "And everything will become clear."

"Clear as mud, probably," Gran grunted, but still did as Harriet suggested. And Shanille had barely launched into her speech, when Gran cried, "Serendipity!"

"Sara who?" asked Dooley.

"I was just talking to my son about this! I'm all on board with your scheme, guys. In fact I think I have an even better idea. You know I can't talk canine, right? But you can. So what I would suggest is we go door to door, and while you talk some sense into those four-legged mutts, I'll talk to their feeble-brained owners—how does that sound for a plan?"

"Are all dog owners feeble-brained, Gran?" asked Dooley.

"Of course they are. If they had any sense they would have taken a cat, not a dog. But let's not get distracted. We need to organize this properly, and we need to make it clear this campaign is officially sanctioned by our very own chief of police. Got that?"

"But why, Gran?" asked Harriet.

"Because I said so," she snapped. "Now let's get going. No time to waste!"

Tex, who'd just stepped out of his office to see what all the fuss was about, saw his receptionist grab her purse and so he asked, "Are you leaving already, Vesta?"

"Of course I'm leaving! Can't you tell?"

"But… you'll be back soon, right?"

"Depends." She lifted her chin. "I've decided to become a cracker, and I'm on a mission—a mission officially sanctioned by your next mayor—Alec Lip. Watch me roar!" And with these words, she left a mystified Tex staring at her retreating back.

"Don't you think Tex will wonder what this is all about?" asked Harriet once we were outside and making good time.

"Who cares? This mission is bigger than Tex. We're about to write history here, fellas. If we can pull this off—make Hampton Cove a doo-doo free zone—it will prove infectious, and soon the county will adopt this new policy, and then the state, and the country! And by the time my son is crowned president, we'll have started a revolution!"

"I don't think presidents are crowned," I said.

"Who cares! I'm walking into the White House as the first woman on the planet who achieved the unachievable. They'll give me medals. They'll give me rewards. I might even win the Nobel Prize. But do I care? Not a frickin hoot! All I care about is teaching America how to make their dogs go doo-doo on the box. And that's good enough for me."

"Oh, boy," said Brutus. "She's as nuts as Harriet and Shanille."

And he was right. It's one thing to tell people to clean up after their dog, but quite another to order them to potty-train their dogs. People have a tendency to rebel when told to do things, but dogs have a tendency to bite you if you try such a thing.

I had a feeling this town would soon not be safe either for us or Gran.

9

The door opened and Odelia found herself staring into Alicia's smiling face. "Come in," she said. "Papa is in the library. I told him you were coming, so you should be good."

"This is my mom, Marge Poole," said Odelia. "Mom, meet Alicia. Jock and Grace's daughter."

"Hi, Alicia," said Marge, who was looking slightly nervous.

"It's so great to finally meet you," said Alicia. "I've heard so much about you."

"You have?" asked Marge. "I didn't know…"

"Yeah, my dad told me about his very first girlfriend, who is now the wife of Doctor Poole, and mother of the famous Odelia Poole, reporter for the *Hampton Cove Gazette*. He reads your stories all the time, by the way, Odelia, and follows all of your exploits."

"That's… so nice of your father," said Marge, who clearly hadn't expected this.

They followed the young woman down the hallway, and into the library, which was, as libraries go, opulent. Racks of books reached all the way to the ceiling, and there was even one of those library ladders on wheels. In the center of the room leather couches had been placed, surrounding a salon table, and Odelia spotted a comfy-looking window seat that practically invited her to pick up a book and spend a couple of hours reading.

Standing near that same window, looking out, a tall man stood, back straight, hands behind his back. When they walked in, he turned. He looked about Odelia's dad's age, but his hair was completely gray, and he had a little white mustache. He had one of those classically handsome faces, that only become more attractive with age.

He greeted them with a pleasant smile.

"Marge Poole," he said, spreading his arms. "It's such a pleasure to see you. And can I say you haven't changed one bit?"

"Hi, Jock," said Marge, still not at ease. "You look well."

"A little older, a little grayer, and, perhaps a little wiser," he said.

Odelia could see how her mother would have fallen for this man. He had charm and charisma oozing from every pore.

"This is my daughter Odelia," said Marge.

"Spitting image of your lovely mother," said Jock, and pressed Odelia's hands warmly. "Alicia told me she invited you, and I must confess I think it's a little silly of her, to engage your services like this."

"Well, she's very worried about her mother," said Odelia.

"I know, and I'm worried myself, but knowing Grace she will turn up soon enough."

"You mean she's done this before?"

"She has disappeared before, yes, and usually gets back in touch after a couple of days. One time I didn't hear from her for two weeks. I'd already contacted the police. Turns out she needed a break from it all and had gone down to the Keys for a vacation."

"Mom would never do that," said Alicia. "She would never just leave us like that."

"And yet she did, sweetheart. You wouldn't remember as you were too young."

"I think I would have noticed if Mama left for two weeks, Papa."

"Well, you didn't, since I sent you to your grandmother for two weeks, and you had the time of your life. My mom and dad live in Montana, you see," said Jock. "They took over a dude ranch when Dad retired, and have been living up there since, having a ball."

"You said Grace has done this several times?" asked Odelia as Alicia frowned, trying to recollect the incident her father was referring to.

"Yes, my wife has a tendency to disappear, just as a way of getting back at me for some perceived slight. She is quite incapable of dealing with the slings and arrows of life. Instead of coping, or attacking them head-on, she prefers to run away. I'll bet she's relaxing in a five-star hotel in Cabo right now, enjoying an extensive pampering session."

"She wouldn't do that without letting me know where she is, Papa," said Alicia stubbornly. "She simply wouldn't!"

"Could you give me a few minutes with Marge and Odelia, sweetheart? There's something I need to discuss with them."

The moment his daughter had left, Jock turned grave. "Look, I understand Alicia is worried sick, and I would be, too, if I didn't know her mother better than she does. We've always tried to protect Alicia from Grace's whims and her many flings, but it's becoming harder and harder as Alicia gets older. I don't know if she told you this, but Grace has been conducting a torrid and sordid affair with an artist I hired to paint her portrait."

"Fabio Shakespeare?" said Odelia.

"I see Alicia already mentioned him. Fabio's been staying at the old gamekeeper's cottage, with Grace sitting for her portrait. Only I think she's become more to the man than just a model. I think they've become lovers, as well, and it wouldn't surprise me if they took off together, since Fabio disappeared around the same time Grace did."

"Do you mind if we take a look at the cottage?" asked Odelia.

"No, by all means be my guest," said Jock. "And if you find that her disappearance is, in fact, troubling, as my daughter seems to think, I'll be the first one to call the police. But until then I'm pretty sure this is another one of her flings that ended with a trip abroad."

"She doesn't, by any chance, have tracking software on her phone, does she?" asked Odelia.

"I'm not the kind of husband who believes in keeping track of his wife's every move, Miss Poole," said Jock with a tight smile.

"Does she have her own car? Did she take it?"

"She does have her own car, but it's still in the garage, so they probably took Fabio's," said Jock.

"I'm so sorry about this, Jock," said Marge. "Grace was always a little… independent."

"You mean unreliable. And you should know. She was your best friend, as I recall."

Odelia stared at her mother. "You didn't tell me you and Grace were friends, Mom."

"Grace was my best friend, yes, and so when she betrayed me, it hit me hard."

"I'm truly sorry about what happened, Marge," said Jock

now, taking her hands in his and pressing them warmly. He looked sincere. "What can I say? I was young and foolish."

"We were all young and foolish, Jock."

"Yes, but I was an idiot for letting you go. I should have listened when you said I was making a big mistake. Of course back then I was completely smitten with Grace. Blinded by her good looks and her flirtatious attitude."

"That's all in the past now, Jock. No sense in rehashing ancient history."

"I know, but look at you now. Married to a doctor, with a gorgeous, successful daughter. You really did well for yourself."

"You did pretty well for yourself, too, Jock. And your Alicia is lovely."

"She is, isn't she?" said Jock, glowing at the mention of his little girl. "She's the light of my life. Grace and I have made a mess of things—I won't conceal that our marriage is a bust—but we did one thing right and that's Alicia. She's our one saving grace."

And with these words, he excused himself and walked out.

"So what do you think?" asked Odelia. "Did Grace leave under her own steam, or was she taken?"

"I have no idea, but I'm sure you'll find out, honey."

"Only if you help me."

"Odelia! I'm not a detective."

"And neither am I. I'm just a reporter."

"With a knack for detection."

"You know Grace. She was your best friend. If anyone can get to the bottom of this, it's you, Mom."

"I can't just close up my library for a couple of days or weeks, honey."

"No, you do your library, and we'll try and find out what

happened to Grace after hours. I have a feeling Jock is right, and that she simply up and left and will be in touch any day now. But in the meantime I don't want to disappoint Alicia, either."

"No, you're right," said Marge as she glanced through the window. In the distance, half-obscured by a large willow tree, they could see the gamekeeper's cottage. "And you probably have a point. The fact that I used to know Grace could work to our advantage."

"So we're doing this?"

"Okay, fine. I'll help you find Grace. But don't tell your dad. He might not appreciate me hanging around the Farnsworths—well, Jock, in particular."

Odelia laughed. "Wait, what?"

"The fact that I used to date Jock Farnsworth made your dad feel pretty insecure. And I don't think that feeling has completely gone away over the years. So I'll help you, but only if you don't tell your dad. Deal?"

Odelia was still smiling. Hard to believe her dad would be jealous of Jock Farnsworth after all these years. But she shook her mother's hand. "Deal."

10

*G*ran had decided we needed to tackle this issue together, as a team. She'd appointed herself the head of the CCREC, much to Harriet's annoyance, I might add, and intimated she would create a blueprint for our first campaign, giving us a detailed script.

"We'll start on Harrington Street," she said. "These people need to be made aware of the need for cleanliness and hygiene and anyway, I've never liked our neighbors, so if this goes sideways, no harm done."

"I actually like our neighbors, Max," said Dooley. "So if this goes sideways aren't we going to be welcome in our own neighborhood anymore?"

"It certainly looks that way, Dooley," I said.

"This is going to be rough," Brutus announced when Gran walked up to the first house and rang the bell.

"So you know the drill, you guys," said Gran. "While I talk to the lord of the manor, you talk to his hairy mutt. It's called a two-pronged approach and it can't fail."

"All right, Gran," said Dooley dutifully.

"When did the CCREC become a human's sideshow?"

asked Shanille, grumbling a little. I had a feeling it wasn't just Father Reilly who wasn't a big fan of Gran, but his cat, too. Then again, pets often take after their owners, or is it the other way around? I can never remember. Or maybe it's just a case of mutual influence.

The door flew open and a large man with a paunch, bald head and bulbous nose appeared. This was Odelia's next-door neighbor Kurt Mayfield. Mr. Mayfield is a retired music teacher, and his one defining feature is that he hates cats. So it was with some trepidation that I now entered his home, in search of the dog Gran had suggested we bring under our fatal spell, while she worked her charm on its owner.

Mr. Mayfield, the moment he saw five cats slip between his legs, bellowed, "Hey! Get those cats out of here!"

A fine start for CCREC's first-ever mission.

"Let's you and I have a little chat first, Kurtis," said Gran.

"The name is Kurt, not Kurtis," Mr. Mayfield growled.

I'd decided to linger in the hallway, to keep abreast of Gran's progress. In case she spectacularly failed her mission, we probably needed to abort and do so on the double.

"Did you know that my son, your chief of police, has launched a new campaign to improve the health and safety of our beloved community?" asked Gran, launching into her spiel. "And did you know that as a consequence of his campaign he requires upstanding citizens such as yourself to adopt a new rule prohibiting the deposit of dog excrement on our town's sidewalks? Yes, that's right, Kurtis Mayfield. From now on, it is strictly forbidden to take your dog out for a walk and allow him to soil our trees, our pavements, our parks and our waterways with his poo and with his pee."

"It's Kurt, and I don't get it," said Kurt now, scratching his shiny bald scalp. "What are you saying, Vesta, cause it all sounds like gibberish to me?"

"I'm saying that Wilbur Vickery has a great deal on litter boxes and you need to take advantage of this promotion and get yourself one of those fine items pronto and then you're going to train that silly mutt of yours to take a dump in the box from now on."

"You're telling me to do what?!" Kurt vociferated.

"I'm telling you that your chief of police wants you to stop messing up the sidewalk with your dog's disgusting crap, Kurtis. And if you can't get that simple message through that thick skull of yours, I'll make it even plainer: stop polluting my town or else!"

"This time you've gone too far, Vesta," growled Kurt. "Show me where it says I can't take my dog out for a walk. Show me this new rule of your son and I'll gladly comply."

"Oh, don't you worry about the new rule. It is coming, and faster than you think. As soon as Alec is appointed mayor, the rule is going to be voted in so fast it'll make your head spin. In fact it's the first policy he'll put to the vote, his crowning achievement."

Kurt stared at Gran for a moment, then declared, "I always said you were nuts."

And slammed the door in her face.

Which had as a consequence that five members of the CCREC were now effectively locked in with this irate cat-hating neighbor, and one presumably vicious dog.

While I'd stayed behind to keep an eye on the proceedings, my fellow CCREC'ers had gone in search of Kurt's mutt, and now returned, their search having proven fruitless.

"I don't think this man has a dog, Max," said Shanille, reporting from the trenches.

"Oh, yes, he has," I said. "He got his dog around the same time Marcie and Ted Trapper got Rufus. It's a happy little yapper that answers to the name Fifi."

I decided to head into the backyard, which was an easy

feat to accomplish, as Kurt had installed a pet door similar to Odelia's. I squeezed myself through the thing—it was a lot smaller than Odelia's—and found myself in Kurt Mayfield's backyard, which wasn't as nice as my own, but nice enough for a man living by himself. You hear these stories about confirmed bachelors: how their houses are a mess, and their backyards are complete jungles, but Kurt obviously was a man who appreciated order and cleanliness, and both his house and his backyard were nicely maintained, I had to admit.

"Fifi," I called out. "Where are you?"

And then I saw her. The little Yorkshire Terrier was hiding behind a tree near the back fence, and just about all I could see were two beady eyes and a quivering snout.

"Oh, there you are," I said, and approached the little doggie carefully. She might be small and cute, but that didn't mean she couldn't also be vicious—a happy little biter.

"There's something we need to discuss, Fifi," I said. "Something that will benefit you."

"Don't hurt me, cat," said the Yorkie. "Don't scratch me with those claws of yours."

"Scratching you is the furthest thing from my mind," I assured the sweet little thing.

Behind me, four more cats had squeezed through the pet flap, and now joined me as I prepared to give Fifi the CCREC talk, as outlined and drilled into us by Grandma Muffin.

"The thing is, Fifi," I began, "that there's a revolution sweeping through Hampton Cove right now. Dogs from all shapes and sizes are taking part in this revolution and joining this popular movement and I'm sure you don't want to be left behind, right?"

Fifi didn't respond, but merely crawled further behind the tree, looking even more scared than before. Then again, if one cat scares the bejesus out of you, five probably are a living nightmare.

"Why is she hiding, Max?" asked Dooley. "Doesn't she like us?"

"I think she's scared of us," I intimated.

"A dog? Scared of a cat? I didn't think that was possible," said Shanille.

"Well, it is possible, and Fifi is obviously very scared, so maybe you guys should back off a little and give her some space," I suggested.

"You don't have to be scared, little Fifi," said Shanille. Instead of backing off, she was advancing on the creature. "I'm Father Reilly's cat, and the Bible teaches us to love all creatures great and small, so I can assure you I'm not a threat to you. On the contrary, I think you're one of the Lord's creatures, just like me and my dear, dear friends here."

"Go away, cat," said Fifi, indicating she wasn't impressed by this lecture. "Leave me alone."

"Look, I'll just say my piece and then we'll be out of your hair," I said, which, I now noticed, was adorned with a big pink bow. Very cute. "Dogs all over Hampton Cove are joining the litter box revolution, and I'm sure you don't want to be left behind. If you learn to go on the litter box now, you'll be part of the avant-garde of a new and exciting movement. For only nine ninety-nine your owner can pick up a litter box at the General Store, and get two bags of litter thrown in. You simply enter the box, do your business, and you'll come out smelling like roses—or baby powder, whichever you prefer. Join the litter box revolution now and be a cool dog. There, that was my sales pitch. Questions?"

Gran had really drilled the speech into us, but I still had a feeling it was lacking that *je ne sais quoi*. Then again, I'm not a salescat, so I probably had fumbled my delivery.

"What's a litter box?" asked Fifi now, showing her first sign of interest.

"Well, it's a big box with litter inside it," I said, "and it magically absorbs your pee and your poo. Pee and poo go in, and you come out, clean as a whistle and smelling, as I said, like roses—or baby powder—but the latter will set you back eleven ninety-nine."

"Why is that, Max?" asked Dooley. "Why are babies more expensive than roses?"

"Shush, Dooley," I said. "I'm in the middle of an important sales pitch here."

"It sounds really nice," Fifi admitted. "I would love to smell like roses. Pink roses. Pink is my color, you see. I have everything pink. Pink bowls, pink basket, pink pillows…."

"Oh, but it *is* nice. Us cats have been using litter boxes for years and years and years, and now it's your turn."

"You mean you were part of the beta test for this litter box thing?"

I paused. "Um, sure. Cats were part of the beta test group, and now this cool gadget is being rolled out to all pets, dogs included. So you don't want to miss this opportunity."

"I think it might be cool," said Fifi, carefully emerging from behind her tree.

"Oh, yeah, it's the coolest thing possible," Harriet assured the little doggie. "You'll be the coolest dog in school."

"I don't go to school, though," said Fifi, eyeing Harriet uncertainly, nose twitching.

"It's just a figure of speech," I said. "What Harriet means to say is that if you become part of the litter box vanguard, you'll be the coolest dog in town. And who doesn't want to be the coolest dog in town, right?"

"I'm not cool," said Fifi sadly. "At least that's what other dogs keep telling me."

"This will change all that," I promised her. "This will make every dog treat you with the respect that you deserve."

"They'll look up to you," said Brutus. "They'll think you're the hippest dude on the block."

"I'm not a dude, though," said Fifi.

"Okay, fine. You'll be the hippest chick," Brutus amended his previous statement.

"I'd like to be a hip chick," said Fifi, now fully out from behind her tree.

She was obviously overcoming her fear of cats, a testament to the transformational power of the CCREC message and the litter box revolution sweeping our town.

Oh, boy. I guess I'd drunk the Kool-Aid, too.

"Will it make me prettier?" asked Fifi now. "This litter box thing?"

"Oh, sure," said Harriet without batting an eye. "Litter does wonders for your skin and your fur. Just look at me." She preened a little, showing off that shiny white coat.

Fifi stared at it with rapt fascination. "You have such lovely fur, Harriet. I've always admired you from afar—ever since I was adopted by Kurt. I think you look amazing."

"Why, thanks, Fifi. And it's all due to the amazing powers of litter," said Harriet, unashamedly plugging litter as a regular panacea. I guess she *is* a born salescat.

"The power of litter will also make you stronger," said Brutus. "Make you butch like me." He flexed his muscles. "No dog is going to mess with you when you're muscular."

"I would love to be more muscular," said Fifi. "And bigger and stronger, too."

"Well, adopt the litter box lifestyle and amazing strength will be yours," said Brutus.

"And don't forget about self-confidence," Shanille told the bashful Yorkie. "Embrace the litter box lifestyle and you'll become a new dog. Gone will be the fear of cats or other creatures. You'll be a completely new Fifi by the time you walk out of your litter box."

Fifi's eyes had begun to shine with the light of holy fervor. "Strength, beauty, self-confidence," she murmured. "Is there anything this wonder-box can't accomplish?"

"Nothing," Harriet assured her. "The litter box is the answer to all your problems. And all this for a measly nine ninety-nine, sales tax included. Buy yours now and get a bag of litter for free. Deal ends Friday at midnight."

I had to admit I was starting to feel a little uncomfortable about all this talk of the litter box as the be-all and end-all of life. Gran had jotted these notions down on a paper napkin before giving us our instructions, saying we needed to drive our point home with zeal and excitement and close! close! close! that deal. But now I wondered if we weren't overdoing it. I mean, the litter box is a nice invention, as inventions go, but it can only do so much. It has never contributed in a significant way to my complexion or the glossiness of my coat, nor has it ever given me confidence, strength or happiness.

Do I feel better after a visit to the box? Yes, I do, but doesn't everyone feel better after relieving themselves of a surplus amount of bodily fluids or other excess baggage?

"I think our mission here is done, you guys," said Shanille now, beaming with visible satisfaction. Preaching the non-existent benefits of the litter box seemed to come quite naturally to her, but then of course she had an excellent example in Father Reilly. By all accounts the man was an excellent preacher, and equipped with a silver tongue.

"I want this litter box," said Fifi now. "Where can I get it?"

"Well, I'm sure Gran will have given your human all the information he needs," said Harriet. "So you can expect your brand-new litter box to show up any day now."

"Um, I think Gran's mission was a bust," I said. "Kurt slammed the door in her face."

"So... no litter box for me?" asked Fifi, disappointed.

"Don't you worry about a thing," said Shanille. "I'll tell my human to talk to your human. And when Father Reilly speaks, people listen."

"You think Father Reilly should join the CCREC cause?" asked Harriet.

"Yes, I do," said Shanille. "I'm sure this is a cause he'll happily support. Now all I need to do is convince Grandma Muffin to talk to Father Reilly and turn him into a CCREC'er."

I was still having misgivings about the whole CCREC'er mission. But then again, sometimes the end justifies the means, and if we wanted our streets clean and smelling like roses—or baby powder—then maybe the CCREC'er way was the only way.

By then Kurt had found us, and chased us out of his backyard and into Odelia's. And even as we hopped the fence, I could hear Fifi cry, "I want my litter box!"

Our campaign was clearly a success.

And the only price was my conscience.

"*L*ook here, Mr. Mayor," said Chase, "you can't do this. Dolores is a hard-working woman and, more importantly, she's practically like a mascot for our police force. A mainstay for so many years she's become a fixture— a trusted figure."

"Listen to yourself, Chase," said Mayor Dirk Dunham, who was a portly man in his early sixties, with a full pepper-and-salt beard and perfect gold coif of which he was particularly proud. "A fixture. A mainstay. A mascot. And I'll add another word to the collection: a relic. Dolores Peltz is a relic of the force, and you know what happens with relics, don't you? They're relegated to the museum, where they belong. But a police station isn't a museum, it's a vital part of our community, and that community deserves a vivacious, competent, attractive point of reference, and clearly Fiona is that person."

"But Mr. Mayor!"

"Dirk, please," said the Mayor as he leaned back in his chair and steepled his fingers.

Chase had decided to pay the Mayor a visit in his lair:

town hall. He now wondered if he hadn't made a fatal mistake. The Mayor was on his home turf, and had the home team advantage. Maybe he should simply have accosted the man when he dropped by the police station, and sprung his opinion on him there, where he was out of his element.

"Look, Chase, I won't conceal the fact that I feel for your Dolores. I'm not just the mayor of this fine town. First and foremost I'm a citizen, and I, too, have known Dolores forever. But that's exactly the problem: nothing lasts forever, son. And sometimes you need a visionary like me to step in and herald in the new. All change is painful, but it's also vital. My niece is going to be like a breath of fresh air to that stuffy old precinct. She's going to drag you into the twenty-first century, whether you like to or not. And speaking of fresh air, have you ever given any thought to your own future, Chase?"

"Um, yeah, I guess I have. I would like to stay here, Mr. Mayor. I've made Hampton Cove my home and I like it here."

"So you've decided to stick around, huh? No intention of returning to the NYPD?"

"No, sir. I'll stick around here for as long as this town will have me."

The Mayor nodded with satisfaction. "I can assure you that this town is fond of you, Chase. In fact it isn't too much to say that Hampton Covians have embraced you and now consider you one of their own."

"Thank you very much, Mr. Mayor. That's great to hear."

"Dirk, please. Now, Chase, you were in LA with our chief of police recently, yes?"

Uh-oh. This wasn't the way the conversation was supposed to go. "Um, yes, sir—I mean Dirk."

The Mayor shifted in his seat. "It has come to my attention that our Chief Alec was less than excited about the conference's itinerary. Am I correct in that assumption?"

The Mayor was fixing him with an intent gaze.

"Um, I guess he thought—well, we thought, that the techniques the conference organizers were expounding weren't exactly applicable in our specific context, yes, sir."

"Mh," said Mayor Dunham, frowning. "You know what I think, Chase? And I'm going to be completely candid with you here, if I may."

"Of course, sir—Dirk."

"Chief Alec has been a dear, dear friend of mine for many, many years. He's also been the head of our police department for going on three decades now, and I think that maybe it's time some of that fresh air we were discussing earlier was applied to him as well. The man is, what, in his fifties now? He could probably take early retirement if he wanted to. Rest on his laurels. Enjoy his golden years with a nice pension. Go fishing. And I'll get to the point here, Chase," he added when Chase had started sputtering muttered objections. "How about you as chief of police? Mh? Would you like that?"

"Oh, but Dirk. I don't think—"

"Look, I'm sure your loyalty towards Chief Alec is highly commendable, but you're young, Chase. In your prime. Just think of all the things you could accomplish. If you became chief now, you could shape the future of this department. You could be its chief for the next twenty, thirty years. Isn't that an exciting prospect? It sure excites me."

"But... I thought your niece…"

The Mayor laughed. "I know what the rumor mill says, Chase. Oh, I know perfectly well they already see Fiona in that chief's chair. But I'll let you in on a little secret here. Fiona doesn't want to be chief of police. Oh, no. She has bigger ambitions, and I want to help her accomplish them. What Fiona wants is to sit in this chair one day. First female mayor of Hampton Cove, and I'm not going to stop her. No, sir. I'll groom her for the job!"

Chase stared at the Mayor, speechless.

"Look, you don't have to give me your answer now, son. Think it over. Take your time. And then when the time is right, you and I can have another little chat, and let's just say I see a great future for you here, Chase. A future with you as chief, and Fiona as mayor. I think it would leave Hampton Cove in good hands. The best hands. Now don't let me keep you," he added as he got up. "I'm sure you have a ton of work. I know I do."

And as he stuck out his hand to shake Chase's, the cop knew he should say something. He should voice some protestations. Put his foot down and demand that Chief Alec stay chief and that Dolores get her rightful place back heading the front desk.

But for some reason Mayor Dunham's intense stare and iron grip wiped all those thoughts from his mind, and caused him to mindlessly shake the politician's hand and then walk out of his office, a welter of emotions.

Dang, he thought once he was out on the sidewalk. What had just happened?

*V*ictor Ball had finally returned home. He'd been forced to walk, as he'd left his bike lying in the road the night before, and Chief Alec had refused to dispatch a squad car. After walking for almost an hour, he entered his home with some trepidation, fully expecting his lovely wife of forty years to have been gobbled up by the monster he met out in the fields.

"Alice," he asked in a shaky voice. "Alice, honey? Are you still alive?"

When there was no response, he knew his worst fears had come to pass. And as he walked into the living room, he braced himself for the sight of his wife's mangled body. Instead, she was waiting for him with a rolling pin, one hand on her hip, the other shaking the heavy pin.

"And where have you been, mister?" she demanded hotly. "You didn't even come home last night! I called the Blue Oyster but they said you already left, so I'll repeat my question, and don't you dare try to feed me any of your lies: where have you been?"

"Oh, Alice, am I glad to see you! I thought for sure that monster had torn you limb from limb!"

"What monster? What the hell are you talking about, you drunkard!"

"I met a monster on the road last night. A vicious beast, all hairy with long fangs and a terrifying roar. And so I ran as fast as my legs could carry me, and by the time I got to the police station, I'd lost him."

"The police station? You were arrested for public drunkenness again?"

"No, I wasn't, I swear! I went there for protection. I figured it was the only place where I'd be safe. And it worked! The monster didn't come after me, as it knew it wouldn't be able to get at me behind those bars."

"I'm warning you—if you're lying to me about spending the night at the police station..."

"No, I'm not, I swear. I was there all night. Just ask them."

"Don't think I won't call Chief Alec to check your story."

"You can call him now—he'll tell you it's all true. I told him about the monster—the werewolf—but he wouldn't believe me. But it happened. I met the monster in the road out near Garrison's Field and it practically devoured me with hide and hair!"

Alice hauled off with the rolling pin and got a good one in before Victor managed to take the pin from her. "Ouch! What did you have to do that for?"

"What do you think? You're still drunk, Victor Ball! Telling stories about werewolves."

"But it's true—it really happened!"

Alice, a voluminous woman with a fleshy face and a firm perm, raised her eyes heavenward. "Oh, why didn't I listen to my mother when she told me not to marry you? I should have known she knew best. And now look at me. Married to a raging drunkard!"

And as Victor took a glance through the window for a sign of the werewolf, he suddenly remembered one crucial detail about werewolves: they only turned into a werewolf when there was a full moon. Which meant he should be safe now. He quickly checked his calendar to see if tonight there was a full moon, and of course there was.

"Alice, don't go out tonight," he said. "That werewolf will still be roaming around."

"Oh, just go and boil your head," said his wife. "Me and the girls are going out tonight. And don't you try and stop me."

"But... It's dangerous out there! That werewolf—"

"Enough about this werewolf already! Go to your room!"

Meekly, Victor did as he was told. He didn't feel like working anyway. His field needed to be prepared, and his animals checked, but suddenly he wasn't feeling so well. And as he dropped down on the bed, he wondered if werewolves ever ventured indoors, and if garlic would stop them. But then he sank into a deep sleep, and soon he knew no more.

❦

*J*ohnny Carew had never sat at the desk of a library before. He hadn't even set foot inside a library before. And he wasn't sure if he liked it or not. Marge Poole had called in a little after eleven, to tell them she wasn't coming back any time soon, since something had come up, and could they please take care of the library customers for the time being.

Johnny had immediately turned to Jerry, who had the bigger brain of the twosome, but Jerry had argued that his big brain was needed to tackle the wall issue, and that Johnny should handle the library by himself for the time being. How hard could it be?

So now Johnny was sitting behind the library counter, staring at the old ladies who traipsed around, collecting books from the shelves as if they were so many Easter eggs, and then carrying them over to the counter to check them out.

Marge had given him instructions over the phone, and had told him that it was an easy job. Anyone could do it. Anyone but Johnny, he figured, as he stared dumbly at the old lady who now presented him with five books of one Nora Roberts, a writer he'd never heard of. Then again, since he'd never read a book in his life, there were very few writers he'd heard of, and all of them were apparently part of this library's collection.

He checked the note he'd scribbled, when jotting down Marge's careful instructions.

First he needed to ask for the customer's library card, then drag it past the scanner, then check if the client had other books at home, then scan the new books, then press the big green button on the screen, then hand them a piece of paper listing their little haul.

So he took a deep breath and dragged the lady's card past the scanner.

"You new here?" croaked the old dame. "What happened to Marge? Will she be back? Is she sick or something? Has she decided to quit? Is she retired? She can't have retired. She's too young. I've been coming here fifty years, did you know that, young man?"

And as the lady babbled on, apparently not expecting him to respond, he watched with beads of sweat on his brow as the PC refused to respond to his scanning efforts.

He checked his chicken scratch, but there were no instructions on how to handle this particular type of contingency.

"Um... it doesn't seem to work," he said dumbly. When she

simply stared at him, her eyes large behind her glasses, he turned the computer screen to her. "See? I'm supposed to scan your card and then your name should appear on this here screen, but nothing is appearing on this here screen."

"Probably a computer glitch," said the woman. "Here. Let me try."

"Okay," said Johnny, sweating profusely now. He'd never imagined working at a library could be more stressful than robbing liquor stores or breaking into people's homes, which was his regular line of work. Behind this old lady, three more old ladies had formed a line, and sweat was now trickling down Johnny's spine as he watched the queue growing longer and longer by the minute. This was a frickin nightmare!

The old lady had dragged her card across the scanning thingy again, but nothing was happening. The computer produced a beeping sound every time the card was flashed, but gave no other indication of what could possibly be wrong.

"If I were you I'd simply pull the plug and restart the damn thing," said the old lady. "That's what I do when my computer starts acting up again. Usually does the trick."

"Isn't it working?" asked the lady behind the old lady.

"Computer is acting up," said the old lady.

"Can't you fix it, young man?" asked the woman.

"I'm new," said Johnny. "I don't know how it works."

"Oh," said the lady with a look of censure that cut through Johnny like a knife. "Where is Marge? Usually she knows what to do."

"Marge is not here," said Johnny.

"Well, can't you call someone?" asked the old lady. "Ask them to come and fix the damn computer?"

"Why is this taking so long?" asked a third lady, impatiently tapping her foot.

"The computer is broken and this man doesn't know how to fix it," said the old lady.

Johnny swallowed convulsively. Even prison was better than this. He picked up his phone and stabbed Marge's number into it. "Mrs. P?" he asked the moment she picked up. "Oh, thank God! The computer doesn't work, and there's a long line of people waiting with their books and I don't know what to do. Help!"

He was having a panic attack. He'd heard about those. You could die from a panic attack.

"Calm down, Johnny," said Marge, her voice cool, crisp and competent. "We're going to fix this. Tell me exactly what's happening. Describe it to me."

"I'm scanning this old babe's card and the computer keeps saying beep beep beep."

"Hey, show some respect, young man!" snapped the old dame.

"Don't call her an old babe, Johnny," Marge advised. "She probably won't like it."

"But she's old, and she's a babe," Johnny argued.

This seemed to please the old dame, for she smiled a crooked smile. "You think I'm a babe?"

"You look real good for your age, ma'am," he said truthfully. "You got a great rack."

This seemed to please the old dame even more, for she simpered at him.

"Did you just tell a client she has a great rack, Johnny?" asked Marge.

"Well, she does," said Johnny. "She's got a great pair of—"

"Let's fix the computer, shall we?" Marge suggested. "Press the enter button."

He pressed the enter button. And as she fed him her instructions, he was pleased to note that they did the trick, and soon the PC was ready to accept the old lady's card.

The line of people had grown, and his armpits were drenched, but he was getting there, and with Marge's assistance he checked out the old babe's books, and then proceeded to the next customer, and the next, and finally, when he was doing customer number four, Marge said she thought he was ready to fly solo, and so he did.

He found that it was a lot easier than he'd imagined, and by the time he'd processed the entire line of customers, he felt on top of the world.

So when Jerry emerged from the basement, covered in dust and dirt, he cried, "Jerry! I did it! I checked out the books and it worked!"

"Great," said Jerry acerbically. "Now you can go and drill a hole. I think I hit a patch of concrete and I can't punch through."

"But I'm needed here," he said. "I can't leave my station."

"I'll do the library, you do the hole," said Jerry, and took up position behind the counter, looking like a curmudgeonly leprechaun who'd just crawled out of a chimney.

"It's not so easy," said Johnny. "You have to handle this computer with care and affection."

"Go and drill that hole already," Jerry growled, and grabbed a card from the next customer and dragged it past the scanner.

The old lady stared at him, her eyes wide and fearful, then said, "Maybe I'll come back another time," and tried to take back her card.

But Jerry wasn't having any of that nonsense, and hung onto her card tightly. After a short tug of war, which Jerry won, he grabbed her first book.

"*Fifty Shades of Grey*. What's that all about?"

Johnny, shaking his head, walked off in the direction of the basement stairs.

He had made a startling discovery. He liked working at the library. And for the first time in his life a flicker of doubt entered his mind, such as it was.

Had he chosen the right profession when turning to a life of crime?

13

"*I*'m not sure it was such a good idea to leave Johnny and Jerry in charge of the library," said Marge after she hung up.

"How hard can it be, Mom?" said Odelia. "And besides, there's nothing to steal, right?"

"Just books," said Marge. "Why? Do you think those boys aren't fully rehabilitated yet?"

"They're career criminals, and it's probably hard for career criminals to change careers, just because a judge told them to. But I think you're safe. Even if they decided to steal a bunch of books, what are they going to do with them?"

Her daughter's words didn't do much to reassure Marge she'd made the right decision, but then again, what other choice did she have? She didn't want to close up the library, and Marcie, who usually took care of the library when Marge was indisposed or otherwise engaged, had intimated she had stuff to do and couldn't get away right then.

She and Odelia had walked the length of the path that led from the main house to the gamekeeper's cottage and had arrived there to find the front door ajar.

It was a small cottage, as cottages go, and she wondered how anyone could live there.

Once they set foot inside, she saw that it consisted of the one space, with a small sleeping loft where a mattress had been placed and where presumably Fabio and Grace had conducted their torrid and sordid affair, as her husband had indicated.

Painted canvasses littered the main space, and on an easel in front of the window a large canvas had been placed with a work in progress. It depicted Grace, and Marge studied it for a moment. "She's pretty," said Odelia, joining her.

"Yes, Grace was always pretty. Prettiest girl in school, which is probably why Jock fell for her. She was also rumored to be easy, which was another reason she was so popular."

"Ugh, high school gossip is the worst," said Odelia with a shiver.

"Yeah, high school isn't always the best time of your life, as everyone keeps insisting."

"More like the worst time," said Odelia.

Marge looked up in surprise. "Why? I thought you had a great time in high school?"

"Yeah, well, I had some issues of my own, Mom."

This was the first she'd heard of this. "Issues? What issues?"

"You know, the usual. Boyfriend stuff, and jealous girl-friend stuff."

"Boyfriend stuff? I didn't know you had a boyfriend in high school."

"Well, I had, and he was great, until I discovered he didn't mind spreading around some of that greatness to other girls he assured were also his girlfriends, and then when I confronted him he asked me to go exclusive, which was great. Until I discovered he'd fooled me again, as he'd made that same promise to half a dozen other girls."

"Nice. Who was this boy?"

"Oh, you don't know him."

"Try me."

"Um, Larry Farnsworth?"

"Jock's son? No way!"

"Yes, way," said Odelia, looking a little shamefaced.

In spite of herself Marge had to laugh, earning her a prod in the ribs from her daughter. "It's not funny, Mom! It was all very humiliating and very terrible."

"Of course it was. Like father, like son, huh?"

"Looks like it." Odelia smiled. "At least we all became good friends after we dumped Larry's ass."

"I'm sure he found other girlfriends."

"Oh, sure. He went through the entire roster, only finally to settle on Janice Cooper. I heard they're married with five kids now. So good for him, I guess."

"And I heard Janice filed for divorce last month, so maybe not so good."

"Oh," said Odelia, surprised.

"Look at this," said Marge, gesturing to a pair of earrings lying next to the window.

"Grace's, you think?" asked Odelia as she crouched down to study the trinkets.

"Let's take a picture and ask Alicia. She will know if they belong to her mother."

Marge glanced around at the cluttered space. It was a mess, but that was probably to be expected. Painters are creative people, and order is not high on their list of priorities.

Clothes had been strewn about, and a canvas had been dumped to the floor. As she looked closer, though, something began to bother her with this picture.

"It almost looks as if... There's been a fight," she said now.

"You think so?" asked Odelia as she dipped her finger into a glob of paint. "Still wet. Though I have no idea if that means anything. How long does paint take to dry?"

Marge shrugged, then decided to climb the ladder to the sleeping loft.

Upstairs, the bed hadn't been made, the sheets tangled up and shoved to the foot of the bed. Signs of a struggle, or a session of intense lovemaking? Hard to know for sure.

She suddenly noticed something sticking out from under the mattress and took it out. It was a phone, and when she fired it up, saw that it showed a picture of Alicia.

"I think I just found Grace's phone," she shouted.

"No need to shout," said Odelia as her head appeared. "I'm right here."

Marge showed her daughter the phone. "How likely is it that Grace would leave for Cabo and not take her phone?"

"Not very. Can you get in?"

Marge tried the usual combinations, but apparently Grace had opted for something more challenging. "No luck. And I should probably stop trying before the SIM locks."

"Let's ask Alicia. Maybe she knows her mother's password."

Marge slipped the phone into her pocket and checked around some more. There was a picture stuck to the wall behind the bed with Blu Tack. It depicted the cottage, and looked a lot cleaner and tidier than it was now. She studied the picture. "I think there's been a fight of some kind," she said finally. "Look at this."

Odelia studied the picture. "You're right. Which means Grace and Fabio didn't elope. They were taken."

Next to the first picture, a selfie had been tacked. It depicted Fabio and Grace, and Marge studied her former friend. She still looked very pretty, even though thirty years had passed. Fabio was younger than Grace, and very handsome, with tanned face and a thick crop of dark hair. He was lying on the bed, his torso naked, with Grace's head on his chest. They looked happy, grinning into the camera like a couple of teenagers in love.

A pang of pity shot through Marge. She'd hated Grace for a long time, but now she suddenly felt sorry for her. Clearly her marriage with Jock had been an unhappy one, but here she seemed genuinely happy. Had someone been jealous of her happiness and decided to put an end to it? If that was the case, there was only one likely suspect: Jock.

"I think we should get Alec and Chase involved," said Marge. "This is starting to look more and more like a kidnapping."

"I think you're right," said Odelia. "Let's call this in." And as she cut a glance to her mother, she added, "Better drop that phone, Mom. This is now officially a crime scene."

14

"*I* honestly wonder, Max," said Dooley.

"Wonder what?" I asked.

We were in Uncle Alec's pickup, on our way to a possible crime scene Odelia and Marge had discovered. Alec was driving, and Chase was riding shotgun. Harriet, Brutus and Shanille had stayed behind with Gran, to conduct some more door-to-door litter business.

"I'm starting to have doubts," he admitted.

"Doubts? About..."

"About our mission. The CCREC mission."

"Oh. Well, to be honest with you, Dooley, I'm having doubts about our mission, too."

"You are?"

"Yes, frankly I'm not so sure if the way Harriet and Shanille keep selling the litter box as God's gift to dogs is the right approach—the ethical approach, I mean."

"I've been thinking, too, Max, and I don't think it's practical, you know."

"Practical? What do you mean?"

"Well, as you know I'm a big fan of the Discovery Channel, right? I wasn't before, but the more I watch, the more I like it. And the other night there was a documentary about the different types of dogs. There are a lot of different breeds, Max. I mean, a lot a lot."

"Yes, I know." I was wondering where my friend was going with this, and sincerely hoped he would get there fast.

"There are Chihuahuas, Pekinese, Pomeranians, Poodles, German Shepherds…"

"I know, Dooley. There are a lot of different dog breeds."

"Well, that got me thinking, Max."

"Yes?"

"These litter boxes, they're all pretty much the same size. Since they're made for cats and all cats are basically the same size. Well, some cats are bigger than others," he said, directing a meaningful look at my tummy for some reason, "but dogs aren't cats, Max."

"Yes, I'm well aware dogs aren't cats, Dooley. So what's your point?"

"My point is that there are dogs that are as big as a cow, and they'll never fit inside a regular-sized litter box, unless they made the box as big as an RV. Do you know what an RV is, Max?"

"Yes, I know what an RV is, Dooley."

"I mean, what dog owner is going to bring that kind of thing into his home? Plus, these dogs—the ones that are as big as cows—when they do their business those piles are huge, Max. Huge! Like an elephant's."

I made a face. "You don't need to remind me, Dooley. Remember Rufus's business?"

"Well, that's another thing, Max. I don't think that was Rufus's pile."

"You don't?"

"No, I took a sniff and I distinctly smelled Fifi in that pile."

"Fifi! But she's so small. She couldn't possibly have produced a pile that high."

"Yes, she could. Small dogs can produce heaps that big, Max. It was all in that Discovery Channel documentary. I wish you could have seen it. It was very interesting."

"I'm sure it was, Dooley. So what's your point?"

"My point is that no one in their right mind is going to want to buy their dog a litter box the size of an RV, and if that's the case, what's the point of the CCREC?"

"Well, Harriet seems to think it's all a matter of supply and demand," I reminded him. "If the demand is there, the supply will follow."

"It's all a matter of money, Max. A litter box as big as an RV is going to cost owners of the big dogs an arm and a leg, and they simply aren't going to be able to afford such an expenditure. The people with tiny dogs, on the other hand, will be in a better position."

"So?"

"So it's not fair, Max! Big dog people will say it's not fair that small dog people spend so little and they would be right. And before you know it, Gran and Harriet and Shanille's CCREC scheme will collapse in a big heap of… um…"

"I think I get the point, Dooley."

"And also, we shouldn't have gone after Marcie so hard, or Rufus, as that big pile of dog dung was Fifi's and not Rufus's."

All this gave me food for thought, and as we traveled the road that led from Hampton Cove to the house where the Farnsworths lived, I saw that my friend was right. The people with the big dogs would never want to spend that kind of money, unless...

"We need to talk to the Mayor," I said now. "He needs to find a way to compensate the big dog people. Make sure their litter expenses don't exceed a certain threshold."

"Um…"

"Taxation!" I cried. "The whole community pays to subsidize litter boxes. That way nobody pays more than the next person."

"It will never work, Max. No cat people will pay taxes to subsidize dog people, and no small dog people will pay to subsidize big dog people. And then there's the pet haters—of course they won't pay a dime."

"Mh, maybe you're right," I said. I hadn't really looked at it that way.

"It's like those electric car charging stations. They're subsidized, which isn't exactly fair to the people not driving electric cars, is it?"

"I guess not." This Discovery Channel was clearly boosting Dooley's IQ. "So no more CCREC?"

"No more CCREC," he said. "Though it was fun while it lasted, wasn't it?"

"I guess it was," I said, "though I really hated lying to that poor dog, you know."

"You mean Fifi?"

"Yeah, telling her that litter is some kind of miracle cure that will solve all of her problems? That was mean-spirited, Dooley."

"That was marketing," he said.

We'd finally reached our destination. On top of the gate, two iron chickens had been placed. Chase remarked to Alec, "I forgot. Isn't this Farnsworth known for his chickens?"

"Chicken wing king," Alec confirmed. "Yup, that's him. Richest man in town, as far as I know. And also Marge's ex-boyfriend."

"Jock Farnsworth and Marge used to date?"

"Yeah, back in high school. Long time ago."

"So Marge could have been chicken wing queen."

"Yeah," said Alec with a touch of wistfulness. Being the

brother of the town's chicken wing queen probably earns you a lifetime supply of chicken wings. Alec missed out.

"There's something I forgot to tell you," said Chase as the gate slowly swung open. "I went to see the Mayor."

"Oh, right. So how did it go?"

"He offered me a job, Alec. Your job."

Alec's head swiveled so fast his neck cracked. "He did what?"

"He said you're in line for early retirement, and he wants a breath of fresh air to waft through the precinct, so he offered me the job. Gave me time to think about it."

"Well, I'll be damned. And what about his niece? I thought he had her earmarked for the job?"

"He said he's grooming her for his job."

"Mayor?"

"Uh-huh."

"So what did you say?"

"I was too dumbstruck to say anything. I walked out of the meeting feeling sandbagged."

"Dirk always has that effect on me," grunted the Chief.

"I'm not taking him up on his offer, Alec. No way."

"Maybe you should," said the Chief now, much to my surprise.

"Are you crazy? I'm not taking your job, buddy."

"If you don't take it, someone else will, Chase. And I'd rather it's you than some politically appointed clown. No, I want you to take the job."

"But you can't retire. You've got a lot of years left in the tank."

"Look, it's obvious the Mayor wants me gone, and sometimes you just have to go with the flow. I can't hang onto this job, Chase. If I fight him on this he'll not only kick me out, but he'll find a way to take away my pension in the process. He's a mean bastard. And if I have to go, I want to leave the place in good hands. The best. And frankly I can't think of anyone better suited to be my successor than you, son. So take it, and I'll be able to retire with my head held high, and with a sense of pride that I trained my successor well."

"I don't believe this," said Chase, shaking his head. "I can't believe we're even discussing this."

"Oh, it's happening, Chase, whether we like it or not."

We'd arrived at a small cottage, where Odelia was waiting for us.

"I didn't know the richest man in town lived in such a small house," said Dooley.

"I don't think this is his house," I said.

We hopped out of the car and traipsed up to Odelia, who crouched down and gave us cuddles. "Where are Harriet and Brutus?" she asked.

"They're going door to door with Gran," I said, "to convince people to make their dogs follow the CCREC'er way."

She stared at me. "I don't think I follow."

"I'll tell you later," I said. "It's a long story."

"Good idea," she said. "I want to know all about these crackers. Now let's get you inside."

15

"*A*nd that's why we think she and this Fabio guy were kidnapped," said Odelia, finishing her story.

Uncle Alec nodded and checked the phone Marge had handed him. "I think you're right. A woman like Grace Farnsworth would never leave her phone when she decides to take a trip with loverboy. But just to make sure, I'll have the airports checked, to see if they caught a flight out of here. You did the right thing by calling this in, Odelia."

"Even though the husband didn't want to get the police involved?" asked Marge.

"*Especially* because the husband didn't want us to get involved," said Alec.

"Very suspicious," said Chase, as he stopped for a moment from taking pictures of the entire cottage.

"You think Jock had his wife and her lover killed, don't you?" said Marge.

"Let's not jump to conclusions," said Uncle Alec. "As far as I can tell there's no blood here, but there are signs of a struggle, so I'm going to let the forensics people do a full sweep. See what they come up with. And now I want to have a little chat with the husband and see what he has to say for himself."

Marge and Odelia shared a look of pride. "Can we come, too?" asked Marge.

"I think it's best if Chase and I take over from here," said Alec. "The thing is..." He sighed. "The Mayor has been breathing down my neck. And if I don't do things according to the rulebook, he might have the perfect reason to kick me off the force."

"He wouldn't do that, would he?" asked Marge, shocked.

"Oh, yes, he would."

"The Mayor offered me Alec's job this morning," said Chase.

"Oh, my God, Alec—he can't do that!"

"He can and he did. And you know what? Maybe it's for the best. I'm sure Chase will make a fine chief."

"But what are you going to do?"

Alec shrugged. "Take up fly fishing? I don't know. I'll figure it out."

Odelia stared at her uncle. It was hard to imagine Hampton Cove without its iconic chief of police. And Chase as the new chief? She was pretty sure he didn't want the job. At least that's what he always told her.

"Look, let's not get ahead of ourselves," said Alec. "Right now I'm still in charge, and our priority should be to find Grace and Fabio. So let's get cracking, shall we?"

"Funny," said Dooley. "I didn't know Uncle Alec was a CCREC'er, too."

Odelia and the others all left the cottage, and then she watched as Chase and Alec got into their squad car and drove off in the direction of the main house. Alec had asked Marge and Odelia to stand guard outside the cottage until county coroner Abe Cornwall arrived so they did.

"I can't believe this," said Marge. "Alec retiring. And Chase the new chief. Did you know about this, Odelia?"

"No, I didn't," she said. "Looks like this all played out this morning."

"This new mayor Dirk Dunham is terrible," said Marge. "A disgrace to our town."

The previous mayor had been forced to resign over a food scandal, and the new mayor had managed to squeeze in the door with a narrow majority. He'd promised to clean house, and apparently he was keeping his promise, only not in a good way.

Odelia decided not to let these events prey on her mind, though, so she crouched down and said, "So tell me all about this new venture of yours, you guys. What's the CCREC and why is Gran involved?"

꙳

*W*e told our story and we told it well—at least I like to think we did, for Odelia and Marge uttered several cries of 'No way!' and 'You've got to be kidding me!' which I took to be a sign our story really gripped. Finally, when we were done, Marge and Odelia shared a look of determination.

"Your grandmother has done it again," said Marge. "She's going to antagonize this entire town, and turn them against your uncle."

"Only thirty percent," said Dooley, "according to Gran's calculations. Sixty percent will be over the moon."

"So the Mayor wants to fire Uncle Alec, and Gran wants to turn Uncle Alec into the new mayor. This is going to be a disaster," said Odelia.

I'd offered my subsidies plan to help support the peaceful transition from a poo-on-the-sidewalk economy to a litter-

79

box model, but Odelia had shot it down with much the same argument Dooley had employed. Those seventy percent non-dog owners would never be enticed to pay for the litter boxes of the thirty percent dog owners.

"Look, I think they'll happily pay just to prevent stepping into dog doo," I said now, offering up my final and best argument. "It's a good plan."

"It's not going to fly, Max," said Marge.

"It doesn't have to fly," I said. "It just has to pass the council and then we'll all be able to walk the streets without being afraid to step into doo."

Marge gave my neck a tickle, which I usually like, but now, in the heat of my argument, it felt patronizing and I told her so in no uncertain terms.

"It's a noble plan," she said, "but it's not realistic. You can't force people to adopt a policy, and you can't force them to pay taxes for something they don't see the point of."

"What you can do is fine the people who don't clean up after their dogs," said Odelia.

"And employ those big dog poop vacuum cleaners," said Marge.

"Dog poop vacuum cleaners?" asked Dooley. "What do they do, Marge?"

"I think that's pretty obvious, Dooley," I said. "They vacuum dog poop. I still think my dog litter tax plan—"

"Drop it, Max," said Odelia. "It won't fly."

"It doesn't have to fly!" I stubbornly repeated, but my humans had stopped listening. They had other fish to fry—or grandmothers.

"We have to stop your grandmother, honey," said Marge. "Before she ruins Alec's reputation and proves that horrible Mayor Dunham right."

"Yeah, she doesn't realize it, but she's playing straight into his hand," said Odelia.

Several cars came driving up, and I recognized the man driving the first car as Abe Cornwall. We'd recently spent a not-so-pleasant time in his facility. There were a lot of dead bodies there, which probably was to be expected from the county morgue.

"Great," said Odelia. "Let's get out of here."

"I'm going back to the library," said Marge. "And hope Johnny and Jerry haven't stolen all of my books and my computers."

"And I'm going to try to find Gran and talk some sense into her."

"Good luck with that," said Marge.

We all filed into Odelia's car, and soon were on our way back to Hampton Cove.

"Um, Max?" asked Dooley.

"Yes, Dooley?"

"Why did we come all the way out here, only to go back again?"

Odelia glanced over her shoulder. "Oh, dammit, you're absolutely right!" And she immediately stomped on the brakes, then opened the door. "Your mission, Max and Dooley, should you choose to accept it, is to talk to any pet you meet, and try to find out what happened to Grace and Fabio. Think you're up to the task?"

"Yes, Odelia, we are!" I said with a measure of excitement.

"Finally a mission that doesn't involve dog dung!" said Dooley, equally excited.

And so we got out and watched Odelia and her mother drive off. And then we began the short hike back to the Farnsworth place.

We were on a mission to find a missing person or persons, and this time it was a mission I knew I could whole-heartedly embrace—no ethical qualms whatsoever.

16

*W*hen Marge walked into the library, she was holding her breath. She half expected the entire library to have been plundered, her precious collection of books having been carted off and the internet computers that were so popular with her older clientele having been looted.

Instead, she found Johnny seated behind her desk, staring into the void with a half-smile on his face. Kids were playing in the pirate ship that stood in the kid's section, pensioners were gabbing and checking their email, and people were browsing the shelves, looking for the latest John Grisham, Nora Roberts or James Patterson.

All in all, the atmosphere was delightful.

She breathed a sigh of relief.

"Johnny, how did it go?"

Johnny started, as if emerging from some roseate dream or reverie.

"Mrs. P! Am I glad to see you! This library business is a lot tougher than I thought. When you did it, it looked so easy."

"Yeah, well, it is pretty easy," she said.

"I think I managed," said Johnny. "I checked out a lot of books today, Mrs. P. For a while there Jerry took over from me, but he couldn't cope, so I had to step in again."

"Oh? And what was the problem?"

"Well, Jerry is what you might call an excitable person, Mrs. P, and when people kept shoving their cards and their books in his face, he got annoyed and started calling them names."

"That's not good."

"No, it's not. He came into the basement looking all upset, and I had to calm him down, and so I took over again, and then all was fine. There's only one thing I've been wondering about, Mrs. P."

"Marge, please, Johnny."

"Yes, Marge," he said dutifully.

"So what have you been wondering about, Johnny?"

"These people, they all take three books, four books, five books. Do you think they read all of them?"

"Yes, Johnny, they do," she said with a smile. "Why, aren't you a big reader?"

"I've never read a book in my life, Marge," the big guy confessed.

"Well, maybe it's time you started, don't you think?"

"Yeah, it's just… I'm not big on reading, Marge. I'm just not."

"Didn't you read when you were a little boy?"

"No, Marge. My pa wasn't into reading, and neither was my ma."

"Isn't there a kind of story you enjoy? Westerns, maybe, or detective stories?"

"I don't know, Marge," he confessed.

"What kind of movies do you like? Or TV shows?"

His face lit up. "I like cartoons. Like that *Road Runner*? Or

Tom & Jerry. I like how Jerry always hits Tom over the head. I laugh very hard."

Marge smiled. Johnny was almost like a child, she thought. And now she wondered if maybe he might enjoy children's books. "I'll see if I can't find a nice book for you to read, Johnny," she said. "Something to start you off with. So how are things downstairs? Have you had any luck finding that leak?"

"Leak? Oh, the leak. No luck so far, Marge. Though Jerry thinks we might be making a breakthrough very soon now. He thinks we're very close."

"That's great, Johnny," she said. The big guy didn't seem anxious to resume his activities in the basement, and she didn't mind a helping hand. "So you like the job?"

"Oh, yes, I do, Marge, very much," he said with a flicker of excitement in his mellow cow eyes. "I think I may have chosen the wrong profession when I embarked on a life of crime. I should have been a librarian instead."

"Well, it's not too late, Johnny. You can still be a librarian if you want."

"Do you really think so, Marge? Oh, I would really like that." Then his face sagged. "I'm not sure if Jerry would like it, though. We're partners, you see."

"I'm sure Jerry will find something to do on his own," she said. "When your community service is over, you might consider working at the library."

"This library, Marge? With you?"

"Why not? I could always use a helping hand." She had to admit she liked Johnny. Jerry, not so much. She thought he had a mean streak, and was very crude. Johnny, her kindly heart told her, could probably be saved. And as she resumed her activities, putting returned books back on the shelves, she soon found her thoughts drifting back to Jock and Grace and Alicia, and how she hoped her brother would find the lost woman soon.

🐾

"*I* don't know, Dan. I think they were kidnapped. You should have seen the state of that cottage. It was a real mess, and then there's those earrings my mom found, and Grace's cell phone."

"I have to call Alicia, she will be freaking out," said Dan.

After dropping her mother off at the library, Odelia had returned to *Gazette* headquarters, where she now sat in Dan's office, discussing recent developments.

"How did you end up being Alicia's godfather?" asked Odelia.

"Oh, Jock and I go way back," said Dan, putting on his raconteur's cap and giving her an indulgent smile.

"He's much younger than you, though, isn't he?"

"Yeah, he is. He's got about twenty years on me. Jock's old man and I were in school together. And we were great friends. This was before he became the chicken wing king, of course, and before I became a newspaperman. And since we were friends, he was the first one I turned to when I needed advertisers for my new venture. He was the first one to buy an ad in the *Gazette*, and quickly became my biggest sponsor. Still is, to this day. And, well, you know how it is. We met at receptions and openings and parties, and stayed friends over the years. I was at the hospital when Jock was born, and became something of an honorary uncle to the kid, then when Jock had kids of his own, I naturally assumed the role of godfather. It was a tremendous honor when he asked me to be Alicia's godfather, and I've taken my duties very serious indeed."

"So serious you were the person she turned to when her mom disappeared."

"Yeah, her dad had told her not to go to the cops under no circumstances, and since she didn't want to disobey him, but still couldn't just sit there and do nothing, she thought about me—and then of course I thought about you."

"Alicia did the right thing. And Jock, I'm afraid to say, is acting very suspicious."

"Yeah, it sure looks that way," said Dan, his expression darkening. "Oh, I don't know what's going on with that boy. He used to be such a sweet kid, and now it seems he's somehow mixed up in the disappearance of his own wife—trying to cover up a crime."

"Let's not jump to conclusions," Odelia said. "She could very well have gone off with her boyfriend. I'm sure Uncle Alec and Chase will waste no time finding out what's going on."

"I'm just glad it's in the hands of the police now. I just hope they find her—and unharmed, too. Grace might not be the best mother in the world, but she's the only mother Alicia has, and she needs her."

Odelia nodded. She hoped, for Alicia's sake, that her uncle would find the woman fast.

"So what are we looking for, exactly, Max?" asked Dooley.

"I have no idea, Dooley," I said, truthfully. "Anything that might lead us to the whereabouts of Grace Farnsworth, I guess. And her boyfriend Fabio Shakespeare."

"Do you really think he's her boyfriend, Max?"

"It definitely looks that way."

"But… Grace is married, isn't she?"

"Yes, she is."

"So… I thought only unmarried people had boyfriends? And then once they're married they have wives and husbands?"

"It's a little more complicated than that, Dooley. Sometimes people who marry have a boyfriend or a girlfriend on the side."

"Like a side dish?"

"Yeah, exactly like a side dish. They still have their husband or their wife, but they also have a boyfriend or a girlfriend."

"But… isn't that illegal?"

"No, it's definitely not illegal, though it's probably not very nice towards their husband or wife."

"They're not going to like that, Max."

"Usually they don't tell them, Dooley. They conduct these affairs in secret."

He thought about this for a moment, then asked, "Do you think Marge has a boyfriend? Or Tex a girlfriend?"

"No, I'm pretty sure they don't," I said. "Marge and Tex are faithful to each other. They love each other a lot so they don't cheat."

This gave him more food for thought, and finally he shared some more of his brainwaves with me. "Are humans a monogamous species, Max?"

I blew out some air. Dooley has a habit of asking a lot of tough questions, and I don't always feel qualified to answer them. "I have no idea, Dooley. What does your Discovery Channel say?"

"It says there are some monogamous species, like hornbills, gibbons and beavers, and others that are not, like the red-winged blackbird or the coquerel's sifaka. They weren't clear on humans, though, but when I look at this Jock Farnsworth and his wife, I'm inclined to think maybe not."

"I guess it's up to the people involved," I said. "Marge and Tex certainly are monogamous, and happy to be, and so are Odelia and Chase."

"Chase and Odelia aren't married, though, right? So they can cheat on each other as much as they want."

"The same principle applies, Dooley. And I don't think Chase cheats on Odelia, or the other way around. I think they're pretty faithful, even though they're not married."

"So… why do people get married, Max?"

"I guess because they want to tell the world they're devoted to each other."

"So why aren't Chase and Odelia getting married? Aren't they devoted to each other?"

"Yes, they are. I guess they haven't found the time. Or the money. Getting married is expensive if you want to do it right, with a nice dress and a nice venue, and a nice meal to offer your guests." Presumably, though, Odelia and Chase simply didn't think it was all that important. After all, they were happy together, and that's what counted. I wasn't going to explain this to Dooley, though. It might take me down another rabbit hole.

We'd arrived at the main house, and, as is our habit, had entered through the kitchen door. It was a large house, but it didn't take us more than a quick visit to that kitchen to determine that Jock and Grace Farnsworth weren't the kind of people who kept cats or dogs. No food bowls present, and no scent of any pets lingered in the house either.

"I guess they're not the pet-keeping kind," I finally determined with a touch of disappointment. Hard to do one's job if the people under investigation refuse to keep a pet.

"Maybe they have a pet parrot?" Dooley suggested. "Lots of rich people keep a pet parrot."

"We would have smelled a parrot a mile away, Dooley," I reminded him.

"I did smell something else," he said now as we walked through the house, just in case we'd missed something. Going from room to room it became clear the house wasn't just old, it smelled old, too, with that musty smell that old houses have. Not pleasant.

"What's that, Dooley?"

"I smell chickens," he said now, a testament to his powerful sense of smell.

"Now that you mention it, I think I smell chickens, too."

"Well, Jock Farnsworth is the chicken wing king," he said,

"so he probably keeps those chickens close by just in case he needs their wings."

I stared at my friend. For all his silly questions, he still surprises me with these flashes of intelligence. "Of course," I said. "He must have his chicken sheds nearby. Let's pay a visit, and maybe they'll be able to tell us what's going on with Grace disappearing."

"I'm not so sure, Max," he said as we returned to the kitchen and then out the door again. "Chickens aren't the most intelligent creatures, you know."

I did know that, but that wasn't going to stop me from trying to strike up a conversation and bringing the subject around to Grace and Fabio.

We set off in pursuit of these famous Farnsworth chickens, and simply had to follow our noses this time, the smell of ammonia and chicken feces becoming stronger and stronger as we set paw for the large sheds where they were presumably being kept.

The grounds where the Farnsworth house was located were vast and covered with different types of vegetation. There were the neatly clipped lawns, bordered by shrubs and flower beds, there were copses of trees dotting the landscape, and there was even what looked like a golf course, where presumably Jock entertained his business clients.

Behind the house I'd also spotted the obligatory swimming pool, but all these things didn't hold our interest. Instead, we made a beeline for an adjacent patch of land, where a large chicken shed had been constructed, the smell unmistakable now. Next to the long flat building, a second similar building stood, which looked brand-new, and also several large silos had been erected, presumably for the storage of chicken feed, and a few low-slung tanks for chicken manure, as I'd once seen on a duck farm.

Inside the shed, we found easily thirty thousand chickens,

all living in darkness, silently squatting on the floor. The smell was foul, and dust and feathers flew through the air, making it hard to breathe.

"So many chickens," Dooley marveled. "And they all smell so bad!"

"There must be thousands," I returned.

A man dressed in blue coveralls was dispensing chicken feed, paying us no mind.

We ambled along, and saw that the chickens didn't have all that much space to walk around. In fact they were packed closely together, looking pretty miserable.

"They don't look happy, Max," Dooley said.

"No, they sure don't," I agreed.

I'd always had this image of chickens happily strutting around on a nice patch of farmland, picking at kernels of grain or the occasional worm and generally having a good old time, but these poor chickens were clearly not having the time of their lives.

I finally selected a chicken that was staring at us intently, and said, "Hi, there, Mrs. Chicken! My name is Max and I would like to ask you a couple of questions if I may."

The chicken didn't respond, and merely kept staring at me unblinkingly.

"Um… the wife of your owner, Mrs. Farnsworth, seems to have disappeared," I said. "Would you perhaps have overheard a rumor about what might have happened to her?"

I was trying to be as polite as possible, but even then she hardly acknowledged my presence. I gave it another shot. "Grace Farnsworth's daughter is very worried about her mother. Any thoughts on her possible whereabouts? Theories? Gossip from the coop?"

"What do you care what happens to Grace Farnsworth?" asked the chicken finally.

I was relieved. The animal could speak! "Well, like I said,

her daughter is worried. She wants to know what happened to her, as she believes there might be foul play involved."

"And what if it was? Would that be so bad? Humans aren't very nice to us, cat, and they're not very nice to each other either, so it doesn't surprise me Grace was taken."

"Humans aren't very nice to you?" I asked.

"Do you see the way we live? Like sardines in a can? All Jock Farnsworth cares about is to make us grow as big as possible as quickly as possible, and then sell our meat to the highest bidder. Not a very nice life for a chicken, cat."

"No, I can imagine it's not," I agreed, starting to feel genuinely sorry for the poor creature. Still, I was there to do a job, and I intended to do it to the best of my abilities. "So no idea what happened to Grace, huh?"

"I don't know and I don't care. And I don't see why you should care either. Though you probably have your reasons."

"Well, my human is a reporter and also an amateur detective, and she promised Alicia she would help her find her mother."

The chicken frowned, and for a moment I thought she was going to pick at me. "Look, if your human is a reporter, maybe you could bring her over one of these days? Ask her to write an article about the way they treat us down here? Now that would be a big help."

I was already nodding before she finished the sentence. "Oh, sure. I'll tell her to drop by. And maybe take a couple of pictures of these horrible circumstances you live in."

"That would be great. You know I've never seen the sun? Or smelled fresh air? This is no life for a chicken, cat, and before I die I would love to get out of this horrible shed."

"I promise I'll bring my human to do a full report, chicken," I said. "What's your name, by the way?"

"I have no name, cat," she said sadly. "Only a number."

"Oh, Max," said Dooley. "We have to help her." Her story

had touched his heart, as it had touched mine. "We have to tell Odelia what Jock is doing to these poor chickens."

I was already starting to walk away, after thanking the unnamed chicken for her time, when she yelled, "Jock is not a nice man, cat. And it wouldn't surprise me if he did something to his wife."

I retraced my steps. "What makes you say that?"

"There's things going on here…" she began. "Things that are very suspicious indeed."

And even though I pressed her to say more, she wouldn't, merely shaking her head.

"Mysterious," said Dooley once we'd left the gigantic chicken coop.

"Yeah, very mysterious," I agreed. "We better tell Odelia. She needs to investigate this. Maybe there's more to the disappearance of Grace Farnsworth than meets the eye."

"Or maybe Grace couldn't stand what's happening to those poor chickens and ran away," Dooley offered.

"Um…" I had a feeling Grace wasn't the kind of person who would worry too much about the fate of her husband's chickens. No, something was going on here, but what? The chickens knew more, but why weren't they telling me? Were they too scared to talk?

I decided we needed to return with Odelia. She might be able to inspire trust in the chickens when she promised to expose their harrowing circumstances. And so I vowed to return that night, under the cloak of darkness, and this time with Odelia in tow.

18

*C*hase was looking around the library. So many books, he thought, and wondered if the owners of this place had read them all. Somehow he thought not. He picked one book from its shelf and opened it. *A Short History of Herbivores and Omnivores in the Ottoman Empire*. Um… fascinating stuff, for sure. Real page-turner.

Chief Alec was studying another leafy tome and grinned. "Look at this, Chase."

Chase looked at that. It was a book filled with pictures of scantily clad ladies painted by some dude called Peter Paul Rubens. They were extremely rotund ladies, too.

"I didn't know *Playboy* published a seventeenth-century edition," he quipped.

"And obviously no fitness clubs available," said Alec with a wink at his colleague.

Chase had been pushing Alec to join a gym, and had even managed to get him to sample the gym in the hotel in LA where they'd stayed for their conference. It hadn't gone down well. Alec was not the kind of person who took to fitness like a fish to water. On the contrary, he'd hated it, and had hated it even more the next day, when his muscles had been sore and painful.

"Must be fun to have the money to buy all of this stuff," said Alec as he picked up a small trinket from a side table. It looked like a green seashell, but exquisitely shaped.

"Careful," a voice suddenly sounded from the door. "That's worth a small fortune."

Alec carefully replaced the trinket and looked up. Their host had arrived, looking as dapper as Chase had imagined, after hearing Marge describe her ex-boyfriend.

"Hey, there, Jock," said the Chief, grasping the man's hand and pressing it firmly.

"Alec. So nice to see you again, though the circumstances are not exactly ideal."

"This is my deputy Chase Kingsley," said Alec, introducing his friend and colleague.

"I've heard great things about you, Detective Kingsley," said Jock smoothly. "You're Odelia Poole's fiancé, aren't you? Marge Poole's future son-in-law?"

"I am, yes," said Chase, "though we haven't picked a date yet."

"They're in no hurry to get married," said Alec. "Young people. They think they have all the time in the world."

Jock smiled good-naturedly. "Well, that's the curse of being young. It's when you get to our age that you realize time is a scarce and valuable commodity. I assume you want to talk about Grace? You think she actually was the victim of foul play?"

"Yes, we do," said the Chief, turning serious. "We checked the cottage where this Fabio Shakespeare guy was staying, and we found both your wife's phone, tucked beneath the mattress, and these two items." He produced a little plastic evidence baggie with a pair of earrings. "I assume they belong to Grace?"

Jock studied them for a moment, then nodded. "Yes, these are my wife's, all right. Where did you say you found them?"

"Near the cottage window. They must have fallen off when she was taken."

"Taken… It's so hard to believe. I told Odelia this morning that my wife often goes off on these sudden excursions and sometimes doesn't get in touch with me for weeks."

"The cottage has clearly been the scene of a struggle," said Chase. "And if your wife had gone off on one of these excursions, wouldn't she have taken her phone?"

Jock nodded. "Of course. That all does sound very suspicious. I'm so sorry, gentlemen. I just assumed that she and Fabio…" He grimaced when he mentioned the name.

"I'm sorry to have to ask you this, Jock," said Chief Alec, "but are you sure your wife was having an affair with this painter guy?"

"Yes, I'm sure, and you don't have to apologize, Alec. I know you'll handle this as discreetly as possible. Grace has a tendency to fall for these bohemian types, and Fabio came along at a very difficult time in her life. When Grace turned forty a couple of years ago she became very insecure. Worried about her looks— getting older and losing her beauty and youth. And now that she's closing in on the big five-oh it's gotten even worse. So when Fabio started showering her with his charm, paying her compliments, naturally she was susceptible. I'm afraid I haven't shown her the love and affection she deserves. In fact we've more or less been leading separate lives these last few years."

"Separate bedrooms?" asked Alec.

"Separate wings of the house, even. The only reason we've stayed together is Alicia, who still lives at home. Our son Larry left the nest five years ago and lives in New York. I'd sincerely hoped he'd take over the family business but he doesn't seem interested."

"You have created quite an empire for yourself," said Chase admiringly.

Jock grimaced. "Actually my father created the empire, I am merely its custodian, and try to manage it to the best of my abilities."

"Don't be so modest, Jock," said Chief Alec. "You've expanded the business a lot."

"Well, one does try to outdo one's ancestors," said Jock modestly. "So what happens now? Are you going to launch a full-blown search for my wife?"

"Yeah, we'll put out an alert, and we're going through that cottage with a fine-tooth comb. Hopefully something will turn up—some clue as to what happened there."

"When was the last time you saw your wife, Mr. Farnsworth?" asked Chase.

"Um… the day before yesterday, at breakfast. We always try to have breakfast as a family, so Alicia was there as well. And then after breakfast Grace went off to the cottage, to sit for her portrait, and I went down to the chicken houses to check on things."

"Your chicken farm is located nearby?" asked Chase.

"Yes, just down the road. I can actually cross through the grounds and be there in five minutes. Though we're getting a little cramped lately. I've been trying to get an expansion approved by the town council but it's a long and drawn-out process."

"You're expanding the farm?"

"Yeah, we're expanding to the north, building another three chicken houses, and a fourth one if we can. A business either expands or contracts, Detective. It never stays stagnant. That is, unfortunately, the nature of the beast, and we have to roll with it."

Chase nodded. He didn't know the first thing about

running a business, but obviously Jock did, or else he wouldn't be as successful as he was.

"Well, I sure think you're a credit to this community, Jock," said the Chief now. "I've said it before and I'll say it again, your chicken wings have helped put this town on the map, and I hope that expansion plan of yours is approved quickly."

"Thanks, Alec. I hope so, too."

"Of course! Who doesn't like chicken wings?" He slapped his belly. "I sure do!"

Jock laughed, but then turned serious once more. "Anything you need from me, anything at all, you only have to ask. I want Grace back safe and sound. We may be going through a rough patch right now, but she's still my wife, and the mother of my children, and Alicia, for one, is suffering tremendously—the poor girl is going through hell."

"Don't you worry about a thing, Jock," said Chief Alec, as he shook the chicken king's hand warmly. "We'll find her for you."

19

"*I*t's an important mission, father," said Gran. "A mission from God, so to speak."

On Harriet and Shanille's instigation, Gran had overcome her animosity towards Father Reilly, and had set out in search of the priest. She was now trying to overcome the man's sales resistance and recruit him to the cause. Seated across from the holy man in his sacristy, which was also his office, she thought not for the first time that it was a gloomy place, and chilly, too, and wondered why he didn't turn up the heating. Then again, to heat up a place as big as a church probably cost the poor guy a lot of money.

"I'm not convinced, Vesta," said the priest as he glanced at her over his half-moon glasses. Father Reilly was a ruddy-faced man with a kindly demeanor and a small tuft of white hair on top of his head. Contrary to what she'd expected he wasn't dressed in a chasuble but in a crisp white shirt, black slacks and a colorful knit reindeer sweater which was so hideous it actually hurt Vesta's eyes to look at it.

"You don't think it's important that we keep our streets

clean of this horrible crap? Do you realize that when people step in dog poo they drag that stuff into your church?"

"Oh, I do realize the importance of getting rid of dog poo littering our streets and pavements," said the priest, "but I don't think the way to accomplish this is by going door to door convincing dog owners to buy a litter box. It's very hard to convince people to adopt a policy that will set them back hundreds of dollars per annum. They can hardly spare a dime for the collection plate, much less spend their hard-earned cash on litter. Do you have any idea how much that stuff costs?"

"Nine ninety-nine for the box, one bag of litter included," she intoned automatically, now well versed in her sales pitch, after having delivered it several times.

He smiled indulgently. "Look, I certainly appreciate what you're trying to accomplish, Vesta, but don't you think you should be talking to the Mayor instead? I'm sure punitive measures are a better way to accomplish your goals than affecting a change that is frankly a hard swallow for a lot of my parishioners and your fellow Hampton Covians."

"They'll have to like it or lump it," she said. "I'm not prepared to clean dog shit from my carpets every time a dog owner comes to visit. It's disgusting, and I'm done with it."

"No, I see what you mean," he said, intertwining his fingers in a gesture of prayer, as if asking the good Lord above to give him strength, or perhaps a way to get rid of Vesta.

"Look, I'm not asking a lot here, father. All I want is for you to join me going door to door and trying to raise aware-ness. Is that so much to ask? And in the process you'll be showing your face in town, and attract a couple of new souls for your church, too."

He frowned. "Contrary to what you seem to think I'm not in the habit of acting like a door-to-door salesman. I have the dignity of my office to consider, and people don't like to see their priest making house calls to sell dog litter."

"You're not selling dog litter, you're selling an idea, and isn't that what Christianity is all about? Selling people on the idea of Christ as their Lord and Savior? Now you'll be doing the same thing, only you'll be selling them on the idea of litter as their savior, or at least the savior of their fellow citizens' health and the cleanliness of their carpets."

"I don't know…" he began, shaking his head.

"What if I started going to church again," she said, "and I convinced all my friends to do the same? That's at least two dozen people on your benches every Sunday, easy."

He smiled. "You have the passion of the true believer, Vesta. And I do applaud that."

"If you do this for me, I'll… organize the next church raffle."

"Mh…" he said noncommittally.

"Look, I'll go door to door spreading the word of Jesus, if you become a CCREC'er!"

"Okay, fine," he said finally. 'You send two dozen new parishioners my way, and organize the next church raffle, and I'll put the full weight of the church behind your mission to rid our streets of dog poo. How does that sound?"

"Like music to my ears, father!" she said excitedly.

They were back in business! She'd hit a couple of snags, but with Father Reilly by her side no dog owner would slam the door in her face again!

"But I'm not going door to door. That's beneath my dignity as a representative of the Church of Christ. What I will do is devote a sermon to the matter, maybe even two."

"One week of house calls," she said. "Seven evenings, six to ten."

"One full day of house calls, and you'll tell Odelia to write an article about the church's need for a new spire."

"Deal," she said.

"Great," he said, and held out his hand.

They shook hands on it, both reasonably satisfied they'd gotten what they wanted.

"You're a tough negotiator, Vesta," he said.

"No, you're a tough negotiator," she said admiringly. The man clearly was a worthy opponent, and a formidable ally.

"So when do you want to do this?" he asked.

"How about we get cracking right now? No time to waste."

He checked his watch. "All right. Let me tell my secretary to clear my schedule, and I'm your man."

She grinned. Now that was a first: a man of God declaring he was hers.

Her day was suddenly starting to look a lot better.

*B*rady Dexter, bank manager by day, and proud father and husband by night, beamed as he welcomed this important customer into his establishment. "Welcome, welcome, welcome," he caroled as he led the thickset gentleman into his office. "You've chosen the right place to bring your banking business," he said with an ingratiating smile. Christian Galvin was easily one of the wealthiest clients who'd ever set foot inside the Capital First Bank, and he was determined to use every ounce of charm to reel in this big fish.

"There's only one thing I need to hear from you," the large man wheezed as the chair creaked dangerously under his formidable bulk. "Do you have a safe? And is it safe?"

"Of course we have safes!" said Brady. "And not only do we have safes, but they're the safest safes in town!" He watched on as Mr. Galvin lit a cigar and was now taking quick puffs. He would have told him that smoking wasn't allowed, not inside the bank and most definitely not inside the bank manager's office, but he figured that if he could stomach the foul stench of the man's Cohiba for five minutes, Mr. Galvin might grace his establishment with his patronage, so instead he just sat there and smiled benignly.

"I have had it with Hard Capital Savings and Loan," said Mr. Galvin. "I was a loyal customer for years, but they screwed me over. Decided to become victims of a heist. Their vault was emptied out and I lost some valuable heirlooms and all of my Krugerrand and Silver Eagle. So now I'm on the lookout for a bank that won't get looted."

"No bank robbers have ever set foot inside my bank," said the manager proudly. "And my vault is impregnable, you have my word on that. Heat sensors, motion sensors, the thickest steel door. The person who can get into our vault room hasn't been born yet."

"I like the sound of that," said Mr. Galvin, well pleased as he took another puff from his cigar. "So can I see them?"

"Of course!" cried Brady, and practically sprang to his feet. "Please follow me, sir."

"I like this bank. Friends of mine bank here, and they're all very complimentary."

"The mayor of Hampton Cove banks here, and most of the town councilors," said Brady proudly.

"The Mayor himself, huh? I like that. I like that a lot. A discerning man, Mayor Dunham. Very discerning."

The bank manager led the way into the basement, and then to the vault room, which was open at this time of the day. "This vault door is ten inches of the toughest steel. Impossible to penetrate," he said as he tapped the door with his knuckles.

"Nice," said Mr. Galvin.

They stepped into the room, where a security guard looked up from his paper.

"Armed guard, and of course cameras, motion sensors, heat sensors, the works," said the proud manager as he gestured to a camera in a corner near the ceiling, following their every movement as they walked through the secure and well-lit space.

"Swell operation you run here," Mr. Galvin muttered with approval.

"You have your own dedicated safe, as big as you like, and I can assure you, your valuables will be absolutely safe with us. You have my word on that."

"Okay," said the man, looking appropriately impressed and distinctly excited. "It's a done deal, Dexter," he said, extending his hand. "You've got yourself a new customer."

Brady Dexter beamed as he shook the man's hand.

"Welcome to the Capital First Bank of Hampton Cove. You won't regret your choice."

$\ast$

*N*ow that Marge had finally returned to her post, there was no sense in Johnny hanging around, so he returned to the basement. Of Jerry there was no trace, so he stepped through the large hole they'd dug into the back wall and called out, "Yoo-hoo, Jer! Are you there?"

"Over here!" his brother in crime called out.

Johnny continued along into the tunnel, until he found Jerry, staring at what looked like a steel wall.

"This is it, buddy," said Jerry, his eyes glittering. "This is the treasure trove."

"Nice," said Johnny, only mildly interested. "Look, Jerry, I've been thinking, and I want to be a librarian."

Jerry looked up as if stung. "What are you talking about?"

"I like being a librarian, and I think I want to give it a shot. Marge said she'll help me fill out my application, and she seems to think I've got a good chance. If you want to try too, we could be working at the library together, Jer. Wouldn't that be great?"

"Are you nuts? We're about to pull off the biggest heist of our careers and you're yapping on about some library job? Once we empty these safes we're going to have to flee to Mexico, you do realize that, don't you? With all the loot we steal here they'll never let us get away clean."

"So maybe we shouldn't do it?"

"Maybe we shouldn't do it? Are you crazy? There's easily millions in there, in gold and jewels and cash! We're pulling this off, Johnny, whether you like it or not. We've come too far to turn back now. Look at it!" he said, tapping that wall of steel again. "Isn't this the most beautiful thing you've ever seen!"

"But… the library…"

"Who cares! The only reason we took this lousy job is because the library is conveniently located right next to the bank!"

"I know, but—"

"Don't you go soft on me now, Johnny. Don't you dare!"

"But…"

"Millions in cash and gold! We'll never have to work again! We'll be able to lie on some beach somewhere in Mexico, sipping piña coladas, and dipping our toes in the warm ocean water and having the time of our lives!"

Johnny thought about the library, then about the beach and the lapping warm water and the piña coladas. "Well, if you put it that way."

"Cheer up, partner! Tonight we'll be rich! Rich!"

He smiled. "Rich is good, right?"

"Rich is the best!"

"Okay," he finally said. "As long as you promise we won't get caught. I don't like to get caught, Jerry."

"We're not going to get caught. This plan is fool-proof."

"That's what you said the last time. Before that nice judge sent us to prison."

"Last time there were unforeseen circumstances. This time I've considered every angle and every possible contingency. This plan can't go wrong, brother. No frickin way!"

21

*I*t was a long walk back to town, and since cats have much shorter legs than humans, it takes us even longer. So we decided to be smart about this and hitch a ride with Uncle Alec and Chase instead.

We could have gotten into the car with Abe Cornwall, but the last time we'd done that we'd ended up in the big freezer at Abe's morgue, and I didn't feel like a repetition of that particularly harrowing experience.

So we simply made our way to Uncle Alec's squad car, jumped on top of the hood, which was nice and warm, and waited for Odelia's uncle and Chase to show up.

And as we sat there, patiently waiting, we suddenly saw none other than the mayor of Hampton Cove arrive, and park his car right next to Alec's.

He glanced at the squad car and frowned, then grumbled something under his breath that didn't sound very nice. He clearly wasn't happy to see us—or was it the car?

He then took out his phone and picked up. I hadn't even heard it chime, but then he might have put it on vibrate.

"Dunham," he grunted into the device, and listened for a moment.

"Look, either you do as I say or there will be consequences, you understand, Winkle? No, I've heard all the arguments, and we're going ahead with the plan as-is. It's good for Hampton Cove, and it's good for us. Now get off my back and do as you're told, you whiny loser." And with these words he disconnected and shoved the device back into his pocket.

He stared up at the house for a moment, back at Uncle Alec's squad car, and finally seemed to make up his mind and proceeded to the front door.

"Who was that, Max?" asked Dooley.

"The mayor of Hampton Cove," I said.

"The one who wants to get rid of Uncle Alec and make Chase take his job?"

"One and the same."

"He's not a very nice man, is he, Max?"

"No, I guess he's not."

I wondered for a moment what the Mayor had been discussing just now, and who this 'whiny loser' Winkle was, but decided it was none of my business. A man like Mayor Dunham probably has a thousand important things on his mind, and none of them had any bearing on the issue we were facing: the disappearance of this old friend of Marge's.

A few moments after the Mayor had entered the house, Uncle Alec and Chase came walking out. They both looked worried, and not at all happy.

When they saw us lying on the hood of the car, they smiled.

"Hey, you guys," said Chase, and tickled us both under our chins. We purred in response, and he said, "Wanna hitch a ride into town? Well, hop in. Your taxi awaits."

"He understands us so well," Dooley gushed as we got into the car.

"He does, doesn't he? And he doesn't even speak our language," I said.

Chase is probably our favorite person in the world, next to Odelia, of course. He has saved my life many times. I think he was probably put on this earth to do just that, and Dooley thinks he might be Jesus. I'm not so sure about that, but he is pretty special.

As we drove back to town, Uncle Alec and Chase were discussing the case.

"Search of her room doesn't tell us a thing," said Alec.

"Yeah, and I didn't get a lot from the daughter either," said Chase.

"Grace didn't get a flight out of New York," said Alec. "I had the airports checked and nothing. Train stations same story. If she skipped town, she didn't do it by train or plane."

"They could have taken a car."

"What car? Her car is still in the garage, and we found Fabio's car parked down the road."

"Taxi? Uber?"

The Chief shook his grizzled head. "Had them all checked. Uber, Lyft, taxi companies, all a big bust. No, she's still here, or if she was taken, whoever took her left no trace."

"Can't wait to hear what Abe has to say."

Alec took out his phone and handed it to Chase. "Here, you call him."

"No, you call him," said Chase, refusing the phone.

"I'm driving! You call him."

"You're still chief, Chief, so you call the coroner. That's procedure."

"You'll be chief soon, son, so you better get used to this. You call Abe."

"No way in hell am I going to be chief. You're the chief

and as far as I'm concerned you'll be chief until you die. Now get on the damn phone and call Abe already."

"Oh, have it your way," said Alec and got the coroner on the phone. "Abe! Give me some good news!"

"No news, I'm afraid," the voice of the county coroner sounded through the car's speakers. "No traces of blood. Plenty of fingerprints, but that's to be expected. I'm having them processed and will let you know if we find anything unusual or interesting. We did find traces of acetone, which can be used to produce chloroform, but is also used as a paint thinner, so no surprises there either. By the way, is this Fabio Shakespeare fellow related to the Bard, you think?"

"What bard?" Alec barked.

"*The* Bard, of course. The Bard of Avon. Shakespeare!"

"I have absolutely no idea, Abe," said Alec. "And frankly I don't care."

"Well, if he is, it would be interesting to see his family tree."

"If we find the guy, and he hasn't been cut into little pieces, or had his head bashed in, or is otherwise engaged, I'll be sure to ask him," said the Chief acerbically.

"Bad mood, Chief? What's bugging you this time? Hemorrhoids? Bunions?"

"He's being pushed out by the Mayor," said Chase.

"No way. You, too?"

"What, who else is getting pushed out?" asked the Chief.

"Why, me, of course. Haven't you heard? The Mayor has been using his pull with the County Executive, and I'm being offered early retirement. They want new people, young people. I'm too old and too ornery, apparently, or at least that's what they told me."

"Old fossils, Abe," said Alec sadly. "We're old fossils."

"Speak for yourself, you old fossil," said Abe. "I'm not that old. I just got started!"

"And now you're done," said Alec. "So who's replacing you?"

"Some kid fresh out of school. She's the County Executive's niece, can you believe it?"

And as the two old fossils exchanged more details about their retirement plans, Dooley said, "Uncle Alec is wrong, Max. An old fossil is a dead thing that has been in the ground for a very long time. Uncle Alec isn't dead and he hasn't been in the ground for a very long time, and neither has Abe."

"It's just a figure of speech," I said. "What he means is that he's so old it's time to put him in a museum."

"He wouldn't like it," said Dooley. "Museums aren't meant to be lived in. They have no showers and no kitchens and no bedrooms to sleep in. At least I don't think so."

"No, I guess they don't," I said. A thought had suddenly occurred to me. Why were the Mayor and the County Executive trying to get rid of the Chief and the County Coroner all of a sudden? And were these two events related somehow? It was something to think about, and I vowed to mention it to Odelia once we'd returned to the house.

---

22

*O*delia had gone in search of her grandmother and her cats but so far she hadn't found them. Gran wasn't answering her phone, and she wasn't at the house either. So she'd decided to drop by her dad's office to see if she wasn't holed up there.

Dad came out of his office when she walked in, looking slightly rattled.

"Hey, Dad. Have you seen Gran by any chance?"

"No, and if I never see her again it will be too soon," said her father, indicating he wasn't happy with Vesta, which wasn't unusual. Tex and his mother-in-law didn't always see eye to eye. In fact it wasn't too much to say they sometimes fought like cats and dogs.

"What happened?" asked Odelia, resigning herself to listening to a long harangue. But her father was concise in his description of her grandmother's latest shenanigans.

"She walked out saying she was determined to become a cracker and that's the last time I saw her," he said with a shrug.

"She meant CCREC'er," said Odelia. "The Cat Committee

for the Re-Education of Canines. She wants to teach dogs to do their business in a litter box instead of on sidewalks, parks and people's lawns."

"Oh," said Tex, taken aback by this. "Well, that's not such a bad idea, actually."

"The idea has merit, but she's presenting it as a campaign sanctioned by Uncle Alec, and I don't think people are going to like the way she'll try to ram it down their throats."

"Alec sanctioned a campaign to re-educate dogs?"

"No, he didn't. He's got nothing to do with this, but Gran wants him to run for mayor, and she seems to think this is a good way for him to launch his campaign."

"Alec is running for mayor?" asked her father, more and more mystified.

"No, he's not. Gran wants him to run, but he's refusing, saying it's the last thing in the world he wants to do. But you know Gran. She doesn't take no for an answer."

"Oh, do I know your grandmother," said Dad, a look of regret on his face.

"She's not picking up her phone. The last thing Max told me is that she wanted to recruit Father Reilly to the cause."

Dad's eyebrows shot up into his white fringe. "Surely Father Reilly knows better than to allow himself to be dragged into your grandmother's crazy schemes?"

"Gran can be very convincing when she wants to be. I better go over to the church, and see what she's been up to."

"Tell her that if she doesn't come back I'm hiring another receptionist!" said Tex as she walked out.

"Will do, Dad!" she hollered back with a grin. She knew her dad would never do that. First of all, he was too stingy to hire and pay anyone to pick up the phone, and secondly, if he got rid of Gran he'd get an earful from Mom.

She got back into her car, and made her way through town to St. John's Church, which was located near Town

Hall. She parked across from the church and looked around. No trace of Gran's car. She pushed her way into the church through the tall and heavy oak doors, and called out, "Father Reilly! Gran!"

No response, though, and so she walked past the neatly lined rows of pews through to the sacristy where the parish priest usually spent his days. She popped her head in the door, which wasn't locked, and saw that Father Reilly wasn't behind his desk.

Could Gran possibly have gotten him to agree with her harebrained scheme? No way.

As she walked out of the church and hesitated for a moment, wondering how to proceed, she saw that a small reddish cat was lounging on a bench in front of the church, enjoying the shade from a leafy tree. She approached the cat and recognized him as Tigger, plumber Gwayn Partington's cat.

"Did you by any chance see my grandmother?" she asked.

The cat merely stared at her.

"Or Harriet?"

This time, a smile animated the cat's features. "Oh, sure. She left about twenty minutes ago, along with Brutus and Shanille. They got into a small red car and drove off."

"In what direction?"

The cat lazily pointed past Town Hall, and Odelia thanked him profusely.

She still had no idea where they were, but at least now she knew they were with Father Reilly, and when she pressed her phone to her ear she knew the priest, unlike her grandmother, would never refuse to take her call.

"Odelia!" he said after the first ring. "What can I do for you?"

"Can you put my grandmother on the phone, please?" she asked.

"What do you want?" Gran's raspy voice suddenly tooted in her ear.

"Where are you? I've been looking all over the place."

"None of your business."

"You aren't still trying to sell litter boxes, are you?"

"And what if I am? What's it to you, Miss Nosy Parker?"

"You can't go around presenting this as Uncle Alec's plan, Gran. You're going to ruin his reputation, and he's already in enough trouble as it is."

"What trouble?"

"The Mayor offered Chase Uncle Alec's job this morning. He wants him to take early retirement. And you're not helping."

"I am helping! I'm going to get Alec elected mayor, and then we'll finally be rid of that Dirk Dunham fellow."

"No, we're not. You're antagonizing people, and setting them up against Uncle Alec. If you keep this up you'll turn him into the most unpopular man in Hampton Cove, and then the Mayor will have all the support he needs from the council to get rid of him. Don't you see that you're simply playing into the Mayor's hand?"

"Look, it's simple math, but I don't expect a reporter like you to understand. When I'm through with this town, Alec will have a majority of sixty percent. And now leave me alone, I'm busy." And she promptly disconnected.

"Aaargh!" Odelia cried as she slapped her steering wheel in frustration. As if it wasn't enough that she had to try and find this missing Grace Farnsworth, now she had to play her grandmother's keeper, too.

If only she knew where the old lady was canvassing.

And then she had an idea, and started typing into her phone.

23

"Oh, thank god, Father Reilly!" the man cried, and practically dragged the priest and his band of associates into the house. "Is it my wife? Has something happened to Alice?"

"Oh, no, I'm sure Alice is quite all right, Victor," said the priest.

Grandma Muffin and Harriet and Brutus and Shanille had quickly followed in the priest's wake, and now found themselves inside a house that was slightly dilapidated.

It had been Gran's idea to start their door-to-door way out here, and then work their way back to town. She'd told her cats in the car that she now realized her mistake. People in the heart of town were all too arrogant for their own good. And that's why they hadn't taken her message to heart. But out here, in the sticks, people would be more receptive to the dog litter message. They were a lot dumber, sure, but also a lot nicer.

And it would seem her theory was correct: this Victor Ball guy certainly was very receptive indeed. Maybe a little too receptive.

Harriet was starting to have her doubts about the whole scheme. She now realized Max was right: it was too much for people, and too quick. These kinds of changes didn't happen overnight, and would take a long time to gestate—years, maybe. And she didn't feel like going door to door for the rest of her life, listening to Gran's preaching, while she and Brutus and Shanille talked to the dogs. Most of the time the dogs they'd talked to were nice, but there had been some specimens that had been less than forthcoming, and told them in no uncertain terms what they thought of the litter revolution.

She glanced around. They were in some old farmhouse, and she saw that an old dog was lying on the couch, resting peacefully. She approached the dog, her companions in tow, and launched into her spiel, even as Gran and Father Reilly worked on its owner.

"Hey, there, dog," she said. "Have you heard about the litter revolution currently sweeping the land? Do you want to be part of the avant-garde? A cool dog? A dog that is ahead of the pack? Well, you're in luck, buddy, for we're here to bring you up to speed…"

"He can't hear you, Harriet," said Shanille.

"Yeah, he's either asleep or he's dead," said Brutus.

Harriet gave the dog a poke in the snoot. She didn't like it when her words landed on deaf ears. "Hey! You! Wake up!"

The dog slowly opened its eyes. It was a large dog, of the Schnauzer variety, and now yawned cavernously, its maw gaping. Harriet reeled back. The stench! Unbearable!

"Yuck," she said, waving a paw in front of her face. "Never heard of Tic Tac?"

"Oh, hey, cats," said the dog, once it had focused its eyes on the feline trio. "Nice of you to pay me a visit. I don't get a lot of visitors out here."

"That's so sweet," said Harriet with a fake smile. "Now

have you heard about the litter revolution or not? The movement sweeping through America? Well, you're in luck—"

"Is that the werewolf Victor keeps going on and on about?" asked the dog.

"Werewolf?" asked Harriet, once again knocked off balance. Once she got going, it was important she be allowed to keep going until her pitch had reached its natural conclusion: the call to action. Now she had to start all over again, which she hated.

"Yeah, Victor met a werewolf late last night. Out by Garrison's Field. He dropped his bike and ran all the way into town, the silly man. Police wouldn't believe a word he said, though, which doesn't surprise me. He's usually more drunk than sober when he's been out and about. But this time I think he might be onto something. I heard some weird rumblings about these sightings myself, from several of my buddies."

"Rumblings about what?" asked Brutus.

"Well, like I said, a werewolf."

"Werewolves don't exist," said Shanille. "They simply don't. That's just an old wives' tale to scare the kids."

"I thought so, too," said the dog, "until I heard the same story from Franky, the German Shepherd who lives next door. His owner claims he heard a scream last night, but he's usually drunk as a skunk, same as Victor, so I'll bet no one believed him either."

"Werewolf sightings, huh?" said Harriet. Well, it sure made for a nice change of pace from having to hawk litter all day long. "So what did he look like, this werewolf?"

"Big and hairy, according to Victor. And with long sharp teeth. He was howling a lot, too. It scared the hell out of him. In fact I don't think I've ever seen him so scared."

"What does he do, your Victor?" asked Harriet, her curiosity now thoroughly piqued.

"Oh, this and that. He collects old junk and then sells it as scrap metal, he's got a couple of cows and sells milk—doesn't bother with cheese or butter. Too lazy, I guess. And he has an orchard. Apples and pears. His wife Alice is the real bread-winner, though. She works in town as a cashier."

Harriet nodded. It would explain why the house looked so dilapidated. These people weren't exactly swimming in money, and if Victor kept drinking their money away…

"Hey, aren't you going to sell him on the litter revolution?" asked Brutus as she walked away.

"Nah. I don't think he's all that interested," she said and jumped up on the windowsill to look outside. The house was pretty isolated, in a part of town that was mostly woods, with a couple of farmhouses spread about. This neighbor who'd also spotted the werewolf was probably a couple of hundred yards away. The perfect spot for a werewolf to roam around, she thought, and shivered.

"You don't believe all this talk of a werewolf, do you?" asked Brutus now.

"I don't know, Brutus. I just know that Victor believes it, and so does his dog."

She suddenly wished Max was there. He'd know what to do. She even missed Dooley. He might be half-witted, but from time to time still managed to come up with an idea.

And then she hunkered down to listen to Victor's story, as he painted a picture of this terrifying werewolf, beat by colorful beat.

24

"*B*ig as a house, he was," said Victor. "And with dark, coarse hair everywhere, teeth like daggers, and eyes red and glowing in the dark. I ran hell for leather and it's a miracle I made it out alive. He was going to tear me to pieces and drink my blood!"

"But surely you know that werewolves don't exist, Victor," said Father Reilly. "They only exist in folklore, fairy-tales and Hollywood movies."

"That's what I thought, until I met one in the flesh."

"How much did you have to drink last night?" asked Vesta. She didn't like all this waffle about werewolves. It distracted from the mission. They had litter boxes to sell.

"Well, I'll admit I was intoxicated, but the moment I saw that werewolf I sobered up real quick! You have to warn people, father. They need to be told. And the police have to organize a hunt. Get some guys with guns out here and hunt this creature down, before it kills us all!"

Vesta shared a look of incredulity with Father Reilly. The two of them had never really seen eye to eye on anything before, but now were clearly on the same page.

"Look, Victor, did anyone else see this werewolf?" asked the priest now.

"Yeah, well, no, I don't think so," he admitted. "Though my neighbor thinks he heard something last night. A cry or a scream, and that can only have been that werewolf."

"Or it could have been you," said Vesta. "Screaming your head off like a ninny."

"Well, I guess that's also possible," said Victor, sheepishly tugging at his left ear.

"So as far as you can tell you're the only person who's actually seen this creature?" asked the priest.

"Yeah, I guess," said Victor. "But that doesn't mean I didn't see it!"

"What did my son say, when you reported it to the police?" asked Vesta.

"He didn't believe me," said Victor, his brow lowering. "And neither did Alice—my wife."

"If nobody believes you, that should give you pause, Victor," said Father Reilly. "Maybe it should make you contemplate your ways. You have been straying from the Lord's path lately, haven't you? For one thing, I haven't seen you in church in months, and I've been hearing stories about your drinking. Don't you think this might be a sign from God?"

"You think so, father?" asked Victor, surprised.

"Yes, as a matter of fact I do. The Lord works in mysterious ways his wonders to perform, and this might be one of those ways. This monster clearly represents your predilection for alcoholic beverages. And what the Lord is doing by offering up this, this mirage, as it were, is making you stop and think."

"Stop and think," repeated Victor, eyes wide now. This was the good stuff right there.

"Stop and think about your behavior. The way you've let

down your community, your family, and your church. Why don't you join one of our fine weekly meetings at the church, Victor? You can talk to people battling the same monster you're battling."

"The werewolf? They've seen it, too?"

"Oh, yes, they have. They've all seen the monster called drink, and they've come away tattered and torn, their lives in shambles. But it doesn't have to be that way, Victor." He got up now, and placed a warm and comforting hand on the man's shoulder. "I'm expecting you at our next meeting. And no excuses, you hear? This werewolf is a monster you cannot tackle on your own, my son. But together we'll fight it, and beat it!"

"I want to beat it, father," said Victor, looking up into the priest's kindly face. "And you're damn right—pardon my French. I can't beat it on my own. It's too big and nasty."

"We'll beat it together. And I'll talk to Alice. We have a support group for wives of alcoholics."

And with these words, they left Victor to ruminate on the drink devil he needed to conquer—a devil conveniently disguised as a werewolf.

"Poor man," said Father Reilly once they were outside. "Sold his soul for a drink."

"I guess we'll have to sell him on the litter revolution another time, huh?" said Vesta.

"Yeah, I don't think this is the right time to introduce the litter box idea."

"Gran?" asked Harriet. "I talked to Victor's dog, and he seems to think there's some truth to the werewolf story. He says other dogs in the area have seen the werewolf, too."

Vesta, who couldn't respond while Father Reilly was there, simply nodded to indicate she'd heard. She glanced around. It was a spooky area, she thought, and one she'd always steered clear of before. It was secluded and out of the way, and she could very well believe a monster could be lurking in these old woods. Then again, Victor Ball wasn't exactly a reliable witness, and if no one but a couple of farm-yard dogs had seen or heard this so-called werewolf, she was inclined to dismiss the stories as a lot of baloney.

"Great," she said. "Another bust. Maybe our next one will be more susceptible to the mission."

"Let's hope so," said Father Reilly.

They decided to walk the distance to the next farmhouse. All these small farmers had dogs, so at least there was a market there for their litter boxes. Now all they needed to find was one with an open mind. And one that didn't start babbling about werewolves…

And just when they'd turned into the road, suddenly a battered old pickup came coughing up to them, a window was rolled down, and Odelia's head came poking out.

"Gran! You have to stop this nonsense immediately!"

Oh, hell. If it wasn't imaginary werewolves, it was nosy parker granddaughters turning up to cramp her style.

25

Uncle Alec had dropped us off at the house, and when we entered, fully expecting to find Brutus and Harriet and Odelia, we were surprised to find that the house was empty.

"They must still be going door to door with Gran," I said when we'd ascertained that we were, indeed, the only ones there.

"I feel guilty now, Max," said Dooley. "For leaving Harriet and Brutus to do the heavy lifting and convince Hampton Cove's dogs to adopt the litter way."

"Don't feel guilty," I said. "Finding Grace is more important than the litter revolution."

"I guess so," he said, but didn't look convinced.

We ambled into the backyard, not really having any purpose to fulfill: Odelia was handling the investigation into Grace's disappearance, and so were Alec and Chase, having the case well in hand, and Harriet, Brutus and Gran were tackling the dog issue.

A sound coming from Kurt Mayfield's backyard alerted us to the presence of Fifi. She was jumping up and down, trying to peek over the fence, and emitting squeaky sounds to attract our attention. When finally we hopped the fence, balancing on top of it, she was over the moon.

"Oh, there you are," she said. "I've been looking for you guys. I just wanted to ask you: what's the ETA on that wonderful litter box? I've been keeping in my business until I can enjoy the full benefits of the litter experience, but so far nothing seems forthcoming."

"Um… I guess that's between you and your owner," I said, a little lamely, I admit, but what else could I tell the tiny Yorkie?

"Between me and my owner!" said the dog, not even remotely as shy and bashful as before. "But you promised I would be able to reap the full benefits of the litter experience. Clear skin, shiny coat of fur, self-confidence, muscular appearance… You can't simply dangle all these promises in front of a dog's twitchy little nose and then not follow through on them. I want my litter box. Where is my litter box?"

"Look, Shanille needs to get Father Reilly to talk to Kurt, and until that happens…"

"Yes?"

"No litter box," said Dooley.

Fifi uttered a terrifying squeal of horror. "No litter box!"

"Dooley is right," I said. "As long as Kurt is unwilling to part with his hard-earned cash and shell out for your box, there isn't going to be a litter experience for you, Fifi."

"But… I need that litter! I need that clear skin, that nice shiny fur and all the rest!"

Dooley had turned to me. He clearly felt for the poor doggie. "Maybe she can go on your litter box?" he now suggested. "Or mine or Harriet's?"

"Dooley, no," I said, and tried to indicate by the intensity of my stare that this was not a good idea. Not a good idea at all.

But too late. Fifi was already jumping up and down with excitement. "Can I go on Harriet's litter box? Pretty, pretty please? She has the most gorgeous fur and I'm sure that if I can just go on her litter box this once I'll have the same shininess and sheen!"

I was going to tell her that this whole litter box idea Harriet had been feeding her was one big sham, but looking into that hopeful little face, and those pleading little eyes, I simply didn't have the heart. So instead I found myself agreeing to her request.

"All right. You can use Harriet's litter box. But just this once, you hear?"

"How are we going to get her across?" asked Dooley.

"Oh, don't you worry about that," said Fifi, and before our very eyes she disappeared into the void, then abruptly reappeared on our side of the fence.

"I dug a hole," she said, panting a little with excitement.

"You dug a hole?" I asked, surprised. How had I missed this?

"Yeah. I didn't want to trespass, so I haven't used it, but I dug it just in case. I like to dig. I dug a hole on the other side, too, and I'm planning to dig another one underneath the back fence so I can explore that nice patch of land behind Kurt's. I think it's probably full of nice surprises."

The only surprise she was going to find were a family of moles who'd come to consider that patch of land their own, and of course the sheep that grazed there.

"Come with us," said Dooley now, as he led the way into Marge and Tex's backyard. "We'll show you Harriet's litter box and you can use it to your little heart's content."

"Ooh, this is so exciting!" said Fifi, her button nose twitching and her tail wagging.

127

"Is it clean, though?" I asked, not wanting to suffer the embarrassment of offering a guest a dirty litter box.

"Oh, sure. Marge cleaned it this morning," said Dooley, "and put in a fresh layer of litter. And since Harriet has been out and about all day, I don't think she's had a chance to use it yet."

"Great," I said.

"She won't be happy, though," Dooley said.

"That can't be helped," I said sternly. "You can't go around extolling the benefits of the litter revolution and then deny those same dogs the use of a freshly catered litter box."

Harriet had done a number on Fifi, and now she'd have to face the consequences.

So we led Fifi into Marge and Tex's backyard, through the pet flap and into the house, where we soon found Harriet's litter box, and watched on as Fifi set reverent paw inside.

She looked as if she were entering a holy temple, or some holy shrine, and it warmed my heart to see the doggie as happy as a clam. She was even singing as she did her thing.

"It touches my heart, Max," said Dooley. "I think I'm going to cry."

"It's all right, Dooley," I said, rubbing his back. "You did a good thing. You made a little doggie happy."

"It's so nice to do a good deed. I think I should probably do more of them."

"You can do as many good deeds as you like. In fact you can do a good deed every day from now on. Just like the boy scouts."

"Do they do good deeds every day?"

"Oh, yes, they do. Like helping old ladies cross the road, or carry their groceries."

Or introducing sweet little Yorkshire Terriers to the delights of the litter box.

Fifi, who'd done what she came there to do, now emerged

from the box. She was smiling from ear to ear, and there was a glow on her face that was nice to see.

"I feel different already," she intimated. "Do I look different?"

"Oh, yes, you do," said Dooley. "You're glowing."

"It's my skin," she said happily. "I can feel my skin changing, and my fur, it's more shiny already." She checked her legs. "Though I don't see that increased muscularity."

"It might take some time," I said, not wanting to disappoint the doggie.

"Great," she said. "So until Kurt buys me my own litter box I'll simply keep going to Harriet's. Thanks, you guys. You're real life-savers."

And with these words, she exited the kitchen, whistling a pleasant tune.

26

"*How* did you find us?!" Gran demanded heatedly.

"I may have had something to do with that, Vesta," said Father Reilly. "Odelia texted me, asking me where we were, and so I told her."

"Nosy parkers!" Gran cried, shaking an irate fist. "I'm surrounded by nosy parkers sticking their noses where they don't belong!"

"Father Reilly, I can't believe you would agree to go along with my grandmother's crazy scheme," said Odelia, as she got out of the car. She'd hoped to find her grandmother swiftly, and was now relieved that she had, before any more damage could be done.

"What do you mean?" asked the priest, visibly surprised by these harsh words.

"She's been telling people that her so-called mission is officially sanctioned by my uncle while it's not. Uncle Alec doesn't know the first thing about the CCREC."

"Liar! I told Alec all about it," said Gran.

"No, you didn't. All you told him was that you wanted

him to run for mayor, and he said he doesn't want to, so you decided to go behind his back and tell people he does."

"Isn't Alec running for mayor?" asked Father Reilly now.

"Of course not! Uncle Alec is not a politician and he's never had any political aspirations."

"Because he's too lily-livered! My son should grow a spine," said Gran. "He would make a great mayor, and a great governor and an even better president. And once he's in the White House I'll make sure he stays there. He's not gonna be a lousy one-term president. He'll do two terms, and if we can change the constitution he'll do a third and even a fourth." She smiled. "Wouldn't that be something? My little boy, a four-term president, and then when he's through we'll keep it in the family. Marge is next, and then Odelia, of course, and so on and so forth. We're never leaving that White House, ever!"

"Gran, you're nuts," said Odelia.

"These are not the words of a sane woman, Vesta," Father Reilly agreed.

"I'm practical and I'm ambitious," Gran countered. "When has it ever been crazy to have ambitions for one's own flesh and blood? Huh? Tell me that, you wise-ass!"

"Look, for the last time, Uncle Alec doesn't want to run for mayor. Being chief of police is what he loves to do, and he's damn good at it, too."

"Odelia is right, you know," said Father Reilly, nodding. "Alec loves being chief of police, and if it were up to him he'd wear that chief's cap until the day he dies."

"Fools and morons!" Gran cried. "I'm surrounded by fools and morons! Well, that's it. I'm out of here." And with these words she stalked off in the direction of her little red Peugeot—actually Marge's little red Peugeot—got in, and drove off in a cloud of smoke.

Odelia and Father Reilly stood coughing as they watched her drive off in a huff.

"I think that's the end of the litter revolution," said Father Reilly with a distinct sense of relief.

"I'm so sorry, father. My grandmother should never have dragged you into this mess."

"Oh, I'm not sorry, Odelia," said the priest as he took off his glasses and polished them. "In fact I'm glad. It gave me an excuse to get out of my church and mingle with my flock. You know, I probably should have done this a long time ago."

"Try to sell dog owners on litter boxes?"

He smiled. "No, get out and about a little more. Spend some time with these fine folk. For instance, I didn't know that people clung so tightly to these old superstitions."

"Superstitions?"

"Well, take Victor Ball. He claims that he saw a werewolf last night. And I would never have known this if Vesta hadn't dragged me out here to talk about her litter scheme. Which just goes to show I've spent too much time hoping people would come to me, while I should have gone out to them instead."

Odelia was frowning. "Werewolves?"

"Oh, yes. And he wasn't to be deterred. Even when I told him the real monster he should be fighting is the devil that lurks at the bottom of the bottle. Luckily I managed to convince him to join our weekly AA meetings. Another life saved. Oh, could you please give me a lift into town? I'd be so very much obliged."

"It's true, you know," said Harriet once they were in the car and driving back to Hampton Cove. "This Victor Ball guy seemed determined that he saw this werewolf."

"Yes, he did," Brutus confirmed.

"And his dog seemed to think so, too," said Shanille.

Odelia couldn't very well strike up a conversation with

her cats, or else Father Reilly would soon be inviting her to his weekly AA meetings, too, but she nodded her acknowledgment in the rearview mirror.

"That dog also told us that the next-door neighbor heard a terrible scream last night," Harriet continued.

"That could have been Victor," said Brutus.

"I'm not so sure," said Harriet. "I'm starting to think there's something to these stories. That there really is a presence out here in these woods, roaming around at night."

Werewolves, thought Odelia with a shiver. How was that even possible?

"Your grandmother means well, Odelia," said Father Reilly now. "She wants people to clean up after their dogs, but she needs to realize it's hard to make people change their ways. The only thing that works is the stick and the carrot. You fine people when they leave their doggie's doo on the street, and you reward them when they clean it up by distributing free baggies. It's a crude way of doing things but I can assure you it works."

"So no more trying to convince them to buy litter boxes?" she asked with a smile.

"It was a long shot, I fully realize that," he said, "but I thought it was an idea worth pursuing. And in the process I managed to bury the hatchet with your grandmother. She's a formidable woman, but prone to overexcitement. She does get carried away."

"That's one way of putting it," she said with a laugh. "I just hope she hasn't jeopardized my uncle's chances of remaining chief of police."

"And why is that?" asked Father Reilly curiously.

"Well, the Mayor wants him to take early retirement, and for Chase Kingsley to take over as chief."

"Ooh, that would devastate Alec. He loves that job. And

what reason did the Mayor give? Isn't Alec giving satisfaction in his job anymore?"

"I have no idea. The Mayor says he wants a breath of fresh air, and that Alec has been chief for far too long, so…"

"Unwise," said the priest, shaking his head. "This tendency of doing away with experience in favor of youth. Youth has many qualities, but we mustn't forget to honor and appreciate experience, too. And Alec has been the best chief this town has ever known. And I would know, as I've been around long enough to have seen how his predecessors made a mess of things. I just hope the Mayor knows what he's doing."

Somehow Odelia had a feeling he didn't.

———

*C*hase studied Grace Farnsworth's phone. Odelia had been right. Alicia did have the passcode to her mother's phone, and had easily been able to unlock it. Unfortunately there wasn't anything on it to indicate what could have happened to the woman.

There were plenty of messages back and forth between her and Fabio, and the nature of the messages revealed the two of them had indeed been having an affair. The last message was sent the day before around eleven in the morning, and was a giddy one.

'Can't wait to sit for you!' she wrote, to which Fabio had responded, 'You mean sit on me!'

After that, nothing. Lots of selfies of her and Fabio, the same kind of pictures as the one hanging above the makeshift bed in the cottage. Some were a little risqué, or a lot. Not exactly fit for public consumption, or Alicia's eyes, which is why Chase hadn't allowed her to scroll through the phone, but had immediately confiscated the thing.

"And?" asked Alec as he took a seat on the edge of Chase's desk. "Anything?"

"They were having an affair, all right, but no indication of what might have happened to her." He placed the phone on his desk and folded his hands behind his head. "Do you think your friend Jock could have something to do with his wife's disappearance?"

"You mean did he finally get fed up with her philandering and killed both her and her lover? I don't know, Chase, but honestly? I don't think he's the type."

"He didn't look particularly bothered by the affair," said Chase. "In fact he almost seemed to condone it."

"You heard what he said. He and Grace had drifted apart, and only stayed together for Alicia."

"He probably has a girlfriend, too."

"That wouldn't surprise me. A handsome man like him?"

"So where does that leave us?"

"I'm starting to think Jock is right. That they eloped."

"Possible," Chase allowed. "But then why leave the phone?"

"She could have had more than one phone. Decided to start a new life with the boyfriend, instead of sneaking behind her husband's back all the time."

"But would she leave her daughter in the lurch?"

"Grace Farnsworth always struck me as the kind of woman who only cared about herself and her little pleasures, I'm afraid. So it's very well possible she didn't spend a single thought about what effect her sudden disappearance would have on Alicia."

"Harsh."

"But in character."

They weren't getting anywhere, that much was obvious.

"Maybe we should search the house, and the domain," said Chase. "Take a couple of dogs."

Uncle Alec got up. "Let's wait another day. She could still turn up."

Chase decided to change the topic. "So have you heard from the Mayor?"

"Nope. And I hope it stays that way," said the Chief with a grimace.

He walked out of the office and Chase was alone with his thoughts once more. He wondered about Grace, but then found his thoughts turning to Odelia, wondering how she figured this whole thing. Odelia had good instincts, and then there were her cats, who always seemed to rout out little clues and hints here and there. He decided to wait until tonight. Odelia was probably busy, and he didn't want to bother her at work.

He sighed, brought his computer back to life by pressing the space bar, and started typing up his report of that morning's events.

&.

O delia had dropped Father Reilly and Shanille off at the church, and now made her way home to drop off Harriet and Brutus. She thought about returning to the office to talk to Dan but didn't see the point. She hadn't made any progress with the case of Grace and was pretty sure that if Dan had any news to spill he would have called her.

And since she hadn't heard from Chase or her uncle either, it was obvious the investigation was officially stalled.

Then again, this was often so: for a long time no progress seemed to be made, things simmering and percolating, and then suddenly everything happened all at once.

She was curious to find out how Max and Dooley had fared, and if they had unearthed some new and exciting clues.

When she didn't immediately find the twosome, she wondered not for the first time if she shouldn't outfit her cats with GPS collars. Chase had once suggested the idea but it sounded a little too much science fiction for her taste. On the other hand, always knowing where her feline brood was would be an enormous help. They had a tendency to land themselves in trouble, and that way she could easily track their movements.

She walked out into the backyard, knowing they loved to lounge on the bench and let the world go by, but they weren't there either.

Suddenly a loud cry of anguish sounded from next door, and immediately she made her way over.

Harriet was in the kitchen, screaming her head off, and she crouched down to check if she hadn't hurt herself. She didn't see any blood, though, or any cuts or injuries.

"What's wrong, Harriet?" she asked urgently. "Are you hurt?"

"My litter box!" the gorgeous Persian cried.

Odelia checked the litter box, but couldn't see anything out of the ordinary.

"A dog!" Harriet finally managed between two anguished pants. "A dog has made a dump in my litter box!"

Oops.

*A*s the Poole family sat down for dinner that night, the atmosphere was fraught with a peculiar kind of tension that hung over the dinner table like a wet blanket.

Grandma Muffin hadn't said a word all evening, and neither had Tex, still sore that his trusty secretary and receptionist had deserted him during business hours, not to return.

"Amazing pork chops, Marge," said Uncle Alec, valiantly trying to break the ice.

"Thanks, Alec. Want some more?"

"Don't mind if I do," he said gratefully, and offered his plate for replenishments.

Uncle Alec has always been a good trencherman, and even though Chase had been trying to make him adopt the fitness lifestyle, so far it hadn't really worked.

"So how is the case, boys?" asked Marge now. "Have you found Grace yet?"

"Not a trace of Grace, I'm afraid," said Alec. "I'm seriously starting to think Jock was right, and that she ran off with this Fabio guy."

"Is that the same Grace you were friends with back in high school?" asked Tex now. "The Grace who married Jock Farnsworth?"

"The one and only," said Marge, suspiciously chipper.

"Your wife's ex-boyfriend Jock, you mean," said Gran.

"Ma!" said Alec sharply.

"What? It's common knowledge that Marge used to date Jock long before there was any mention of Tex."

Dooley and I, who were lying on the carpet, shared a look of concern. Marge had specifically asked Odelia not to mention that she'd gone out to the Farnsworth house that morning, so as not to make her husband jealous, but she hadn't told Gran, which she probably should have.

"So did you and Odelia find something at the Farnsworth cottage this morning?" Gran now asked. "I'll bet Jock was happy to see you, huh? I'll bet he's still got the hots for you."

Tex looked up as if stung. "You went to see Jock Farnsworth this morning?"

"Well, Alicia asked for our help, so…"

"Who's Alicia? "asked Tex suspiciously.

"She's Grace and Jock's daughter," said Odelia, "and also Dan's goddaughter. So when her mother went missing she turned first to her father, but he claimed Grace was probably on holiday and had neglected to tell her daughter. Alicia didn't buy that explanation, so she turned to her godfather for help, and then Dan asked me, and then I asked Mom to make the necessary introductions."

"So you met Jock," said Tex, staring down at a big glob of mayonnaise. He'd dabbed his index finger in the glob and was making circular motions for some reason.

"Tex is playing with his food. Marge isn't going to like that," said Dooley.

"I think that's probably the furthest thing from her mind right now," I said.

"Oh, honey, don't be upset," said Marge, placing a hand on her husband's arm. He jerked it away.

"So did you and Jock have a good time? Reminisce? Talk about the good old days?"

"Oh, Dad, don't be that way," said Odelia.

"Yeah, Tex, don't be an asshole," said Gran.

But Tex's face had taken on a mutinous expression. "Thank you all for your concern, but I just lost my appetite." And with these words he pushed back his chair, got up, and walked off.

"I guess he didn't like those pork chops," said Alec, untroubled by the events that had just transpired. He eyed his brother-in-law's plate. Marge took it and handed it to him.

"Thanks, honey," said Alec. "Sure he doesn't want them anymore?"

"Pretty sure," said Marge.

"Why is Tex behaving like a moron?" asked Gran.

"Oh, Ma, please," said Marge, and also left the table.

Now it was just Gran, Alec, Chase and Odelia. And Dooley and me under the table.

"He can't possibly still be jealous after thirty years, can he?" said Gran. "Only an idiot would feel threatened by a boyfriend who dumped Marge three decades ago."

"Tex has always felt threatened by Jock," said Uncle Alec. "And why not? Jock is successful, rich and handsome. And Tex always felt he played second fiddle to the guy, and that Marge only picked him because she couldn't have Jock. So she settled for less."

"Tex was the rebound guy?" asked Gran.

Alec nodded. "At first I think he was, and it's always made him feel insecure. Tex has never been Mr. Popular the way Jock was. Jock was the kid all the girls wanted to be with, the kid all the boys wanted to be. And so when Marge got dumped, and hooked up with Tex, he was always looking over his shoulder, afraid Jock would decide to take her back."

"She would never have done that, would she?" asked Odelia.

"I'm not sure. She took it pretty hard when Jock dumped her for Grace," said Alec, "especially since Grace held onto him, and eventually married the guy. Marge probably wondered why she hadn't been able to do that, and what Grace had that she didn't have. But I say it was all for the best. Tex is ten times the man Jock Farnsworth is, and I'm sure Jock would never have been able to make Marge happy the way Tex has."

"A pity he doesn't realize that himself," said Odelia.

"Yeah, but isn't that always the way, though?" asked Chase. "The best guys don't realize their own value?"

"I realize how valuable you are," said Odelia, smiling at her boyfriend. "And how lucky I am."

"No I'm the lucky one," he said.

"No, I'm the lucky one."

"Oh, can you two lovebirds go and coo somewhere else?" said Gran. "It's making me sick to the stomach."

"Gran is in a great mood," said Dooley.

"Gran is always in a great mood," I said.

"So how about your litter box revolution, Gran?" asked Odelia. "Are you still going through with it?"

"I dropped it," said Gran morosely. "Because of a certain nosy parker who decided to show up unannounced and uninvited."

"I told you, you can't go around telling people to buy litter boxes and make it sound as if Uncle Alec ordered them to."

"Wait, what?" asked Alec. "She did what now?"

"Gran went door to door today with Father Reilly and Harriet and Brutus and Shanille," said Odelia with a smile, as

Gran rolled her eyes. "She tried to sell dog owners on the litter box revolution and told them you sanctioned a new rule whereby they're not allowed to let their dogs do their business on the sidewalk and have to train them to use a litter box."

"You told them I said that?" asked Alec, replacing his pork chop on his plate. It was a testament to his extreme emotion. Under normal circumstances Alec would never put down a pork chop once he's targeted it for consumption.

"I wanted to boost your candidacy!" said Gran. "At thirty percent dog owners are a minority in this town, like I told you, and so sixty percent of the population would be happy they didn't have to step in dog shit anymore—giving you a nice fat majority."

"I think that's seventy percent, Vesta," said Chase.

"Who asked you, mathlete wannabe?!"

"But I told you I don't want to run for mayor!" said Alec.

"You don't know what's good for you, Alec. You never did. You need your mother to decide for you—always have!"

"No, I don't! I like being chief. I want to be chief. I want to keep on being chief!"

"Not for much longer, you won't," said Chase.

"Exactly!" said Gran. "If you want to keep on being chief, you need to get rid of this mayor! And the only way to do that is by running for mayor yourself. That way you can appoint yourself chief."

"I can't be mayor and chief, Ma."

"Yes, you can. It's called multi-tasking and people do it every day. Just look at Jeff Bezos. He's CEO *and* hot stud muffin at the same time. And if Jeff can do it, you can, too!"

Alec was shaking his head, then pushed himself away from the table and got up. "I'm going home to watch the game. Are you coming, Chase?"

"You can watch it at my place," said Odelia.

"Are you going out?" asked Chase.

"Yes, I am," said Odelia, giving me and Dooley a wink. "I have some unfinished business involving chickens."

29

"Oh, honey, don't be upset," said Marge as she tried to talk her unresponsive husband off the proverbial ledge. "You know I only went down there because Odelia asked me to. I haven't thought about Jock in many, many years."

But Tex was staring at the TV, where some Netflix horror movie was playing, a genre he normally hated. His face had taken on a rebellious expression and he was sitting with his arms folded across his chest.

"You can't still be jealous of Jock after all these years. Do you really think I would have married you if I loved Jock? You're crazy if you think that."

"Jock calls and immediately you go running," said Tex. "That tells me everything I need to know."

"I didn't go running because Jock called. I went because Odelia asked me to. What did you want me to do? Tell her I couldn't go because it would make you upset?"

"I'm not upset," he grunted, looking extremely upset.

She laughed. "Oh, Mr. Grumpy McGrumpypants. I only love you, Tex, and have loved you for thirty years now. Yes, I was in love with Jock back in high school, or at least I thought I was, but that was just a schoolgirl crush. And it's also true I was sad when he left me for Grace, but then I met you, and I soon realized Jock had done me a huge favor. If he hadn't dumped me I wouldn't have fallen for you, and we wouldn't have made this wonderful life together, and had this amazing daughter."

"You fell for me?" he asked in a small voice.

"Of course I did!"

"I wasn't just some… rebound guy?"

"Of course not! By the time I met you I'd long forgotten about Jock. I was over him."

"I didn't know that," he said. "I always assumed you only hooked up with me so you could show off to Jock—make him jealous."

"Oh, Tex," she said, and looped her arm through his. He let her, and gave her his best lost puppy look.

"Vesta's right. I'm an idiot."

"Yes, you are, but you're my idiot," she said, nestling against his chest.

"I'm sorry, Marge. I've behaved like a silly school kid."

"Yes, you did, and you didn't finish your pork chop."

"I'm hungry," he said now.

"I think my brother ate your pork chop."

"Of course he did."

She laughed. "What is this stuff you're watching?"

"I don't know but it's terrible!"

Now they both laughed, and kissed.

"I'm sorry," he said finally. "I guess sometimes I still feel I'm not good enough for you. I wonder from time to time why you picked me, and how I ever got to be so lucky."

"I picked you because I love you, and that hasn't changed in all these years. In fact I might love you even more now than I did when we first met."

"You do?"

"Yes, I do."

"I do, too," he murmured, and then they kissed again.

Vesta, who'd come into the living room to watch some television, grunted, "Oh, get a room," and walked out again.

❧

"*I* think this is it, Jer," said Johnny.

"I think you're right, Johnny," said Jerry.

They'd just managed to cut a nice hole in the steel plate, and were now waiting for the smoke to clear and the metal to cool off. Johnny had slid up the goggles he used when handling the blowtorch, and waited with bated breath for the result of his efforts.

Finally Jerry decided the coast was clear, and stuck his hand in. When he pulled it out again, it wasn't filled with gold or coins or even jewels. Instead, he was grasping a big brown paper envelope, and stared at it, an expression of annoyance on his ferrety face.

He then stuck his hand back in and searched around.

Nothing.

"It's empty!" he cried, aghast.

"What's in the envelope?" asked Johnny.

"Who cares! It can't be gold or cash!"

"Could be bearer bonds or checks."

With a growl, Jerry tore open the envelope. It contained a sheaf of papers. Scanning the first page, he frowned. "It's a contract. A contract! Who keeps contracts in their safe! Of all the stupid…"

And he was about to tear the contract into little pieces when Johnny took them from his hands. He studied them carefully. "Hey, Jer, this must be the Mayor's safe. It says here Dirk Dunham. Isn't that the name of the new mayor?"

"Who cares? It's just a stupid document! Let's do the next one. Come on!"

Johnny nodded and did as he was told, but as he thought about the contract, an idea started to creep into his mind. It wasn't a fully formed idea, but the seed of an idea. It would take a little time before it grew into an actual notion, but as he lowered the safety goggles over his eyes and lit up the blowtorch, it was gestating away in that big head of his.

He had a feeling it was a good idea—a super idea—but couldn't quite grasp it yet.

30

*O*delia had parked her pickup down the road from the Farnsworth house. I'd told her how to get to the chicken shed, and she'd listened carefully.

She now pulled a black mask over her face, two holes where her eyes were, and Dooley and I stared at her.

"What's with the mask?" I asked.

"Duh. So people won't recognize me, of course."

"Oh," I said. "Of course."

"You look like a crook," Dooley laughed.

"You look like a bank robber," Brutus grinned.

"You look like a monster," Harriet giggled.

"I look like a person who doesn't want to get caught trespassing," said Odelia, and got out, then opened the back door for us so we could do the same. "Now listen to me very carefully. If by some unfortunate circumstance I should get caught, you run like the wind, you hear me? You don't let these people catch you."

"But you're not going to get caught, are you, Odelia?" said Dooley, a note of worry in his voice. "I mean, you're wearing the mask, so you can't get caught, right?"

"Oh, Dooley," said Harriet. "That mask isn't going to prevent her from getting caught."

"Oh," said Dooley, processing this nugget of information. "So maybe you shouldn't wear it?"

"Let's get going," said Odelia, who was done wasting time explaining the hows and whys of this most important chicken mission. She'd brought her camera, so she could snap pictures of the chickens, and even shoot a video.

So we all set paw for the chicken shed, and followed Odelia's instructions, which were to keep quiet until we got to our destination. But of course those instructions had fallen on deaf ears with Harriet.

"I still don't understand why you told Fifi she could use my litter box," she said now.

"Because she asked us to," said Dooley, "and she looked so sad."

"That's still no reason to let her take a huge dump in my litter box. Now Marge had to go and change all of my litter again."

"But why?" I asked. "She just changed it this morning."

"I'm not going on a litter box that has been used by a *dog*!" said Harriet indignantly.

"It was just the one little doo-doo," said Dooley.

"Oh, no, it wasn't. You should have seen that doo-doo. It was a gigantic pile of doo-doo. I didn't even know a tiny dog like Fifi could produce a doo-doo that big."

"She'd been keeping it in," I said, "so she probably saved up."

"Well, she was happy," said Dooley. "And isn't that what life is all about, doing little favors here and there, carrying old ladies' groceries and making dogs happy?"

"Besides, you made that dog a lot of promises, Harriet," I pointed out. "You said litter would make her skin glow, and her fur nice and shiny like yours."

"That's sales talk!" said Harriet. "Everybody knows sales talk is a bunch of baloney."

"Fifi doesn't know. She believed everything you told her."

"She was really looking forward to all that muscularity," said Dooley.

"I probably shouldn't have told her that," Brutus grunted. "I guess I got carried away."

"Yes, you did," I said. "And so did you, Harriet. You promised that poor dog all kinds of things litter simply can't deliver, and now she's going to be disappointed when it doesn't come to pass, and then what?"

"You're meowing up the wrong tree here, Max," said Harriet. "Gran provided us with the script for these sales pitches, remember? She fed us these lines."

"You can't blame this on Gran, Harriet. You have a responsibility, and I think you should apologize to Fifi."

"Me! Apologize to her! She should apologize to me for using my litter box!"

"Shush, you guys," said Odelia. "We're almost there!"

We'd been traipsing along the road, and had now arrived at the entrance to the Farnsworth chicken farm—or factory. I couldn't see a lot of security, but then that's probably the point of security: to make sure you don't see them until they see you.

I hoped Odelia wouldn't get caught, though. I didn't think that would go down well with Jock. During the daytime she was helping him find his wife, and at night she was sneaking around his property. Not a good look.

She was leading the charge now, jumping over a small creek, then getting down into the long grass on the other side, and scanning the place. When she decided the coast was clear, and our cat's eyes didn't spot any sign of life either, she proceeded, staying low. We'd reached the large shed, and she ran straight out to the door, then looked inside.

Chickens were softly clucking, and she stuck up her thumb, then stealthily proceeded inside. We followed in her wake, and found ourselves in a different, more horrible world.

The stench of ammonia and chicken dung was overpowering, and I felt nauseous.

"Now I understand why Odelia is wearing that mask!" said Harriet. "Not for the guards but for the stench!"

"Maybe we should wear masks," said Dooley now. "So we don't get recognized."

Thirty thousand chickens sat cooped up inside the long chicken house, and Odelia immediately started snapping pictures.

I proceeded along, in search of the chicken we'd made the acquaintance of that morning. It was hard to find her, amidst thousands of her sisters, but finally I managed.

"Oh, hey, there," she said. "I thought you'd forgotten all about me."

"Of course not," I said. "So this is our human, Odelia. As I told you, she's a reporter, and she's here to write a story about the way you guys are being treated in here."

And as the chicken told her tale of woe, and Odelia carefully listened to my translation, and jotted everything down, Harriet and Brutus and Dooley spread out, and checked out the rest of the chicken shed. There wasn't a lot to see, but Harriet had had this idea that Jock might have killed his wife and her lover, and fed her to his chickens, so she was adamant to prove her theory right.

I'd told her people didn't feed bodies of murdered spouses to their chickens but to their pigs, but of course she wouldn't listen, as usual.

And just when Odelia was rounding up her visit, having shot a little video of the circumstances in which these poor animals had to live, suddenly a voice rang out.

"Hey! What are you doing!"

It was one of the workers, carrying a bucket, which he now dropped as he came rushing towards us.

"Time to go!" said Odelia, and was off like a rocket!

"Harriet! Brutus! Dooley!" I bellowed, but the chickens had been stirred up by the shouts, and were flapping their wings and clucking loudly, drowning out my shouts.

So I decided to paw it, too, if I didn't want to get caught by this man, who looked very annoyed indeed. I also saw he'd picked up a weapon in the form of a pitchfork, and if there's one thing that gives me nightmares, it's to become the victim of a pitchfork attack!

So I ran and ran and ran, until I'd reached that creek, and only then did I look back.

I'm not really built for running, I have to admit, so I was panting pretty heavily. Odelia had already vaulted across the creek, and now urged me to do the same.

"But the others are still back there!" I said.

"Don't worry about them. They're smart. They'll have gotten out," she said.

I made the jump, but all that running had worn me out, and I landed in the middle of the creek. Eek! Lucky for me, Odelia immediately grabbed me by the neck and fished me out.

"You're heavy, Max," she grunted.

"It's all that water," I said. "I'm like a sponge. I soak it all up."

"We'll have to teach you how to swim one of these days," she said as she took off her mask and used it to rub me down.

When she was done, I shook myself, but now felt thoroughly annoyed. Running, swimming, what was next? Riding a bike? This was starting to feel like a triathlon!

I shouldn't have worried about my friends, though, for

they soon met up with us, having escaped through a different exit.

"And?" asked Dooley. "What did you think?"

Odelia looked grim. "I had no idea," she said. "It's horrible what Jock is doing. Absolutely terrible."

It was clear Jock stock was trading at an absolute low.

Just about as low as it could possibly go, in fact.

And it served him right, too.

31

*W*e'd been walking back to the car when I suddenly heard a loud and piercing scream, followed by a terrifying roar!

We all halted in our tracks, and looked in the direction the sounds were coming from.

"The werewolf!" Dooley said. "It came back!"

"Werewolves don't exist," Dooley, said Odelia, but her words lacked conviction.

We were close to the car, and could have easily made the run to safety, but instead, Odelia hesitated. It's the curse of the reporter: they do put themselves in the most terrible situations, simply to satisfy that insatiable curiosity.

"Werewolves don't exist," she repeated, more to herself than to us. "Which means that's not a werewolf but some other beast, or maybe even a man. Which means…" She fingered her camera longingly.

"No, Odelia," I told her. "No way. That's clearly some wild and extremely dangerous animal, and we should run away from danger, not towards it."

"If I could only snap a picture of this creature…" she began.

"No, Odelia!" we all yelled in chorus.

"But just think, you guys! Tomorrow's front page, featuring a picture of the beast."

"Featuring our obituaries, you mean," Brutus murmured.

"No," I said, making my meaning perfectly clear. "And no means no."

And then, of course, the beast suddenly came crashing through the undergrowth and we stood face to face with it.

It was huge, as Victor Ball had indicated, and hairy and horrifying. It had long fangs that were dripping with saliva, catching the light of the full moon, and its eyes were red and menacing. Its claws were also dripping, and I realized they were probably dripping with blood! The monster had already made one victim, and now it was about to add us to the list, mere notches on its sizable belt—if werewolves wear belts, of course.

But what did Odelia do? Instead of turning and running away, she took out her camera and started snapping shots of the vile and hideous creature!

It's the same way with war reporters. The moment a bomb goes off, do they run and hide? No, they start taking pictures.

"Odelia!" I cried. "Run!"

Harriet and Brutus and Dooley hadn't waited for my instructions. They were already running full tilt in the direction of the car.

"Look at the thing, Max," said Odelia, sounding excited rather than scared. "It's so big and scary!"

The beast suddenly roared, showing its fangs and pawing the air with its claws of steel.

And then it was charging towards us!

"Odelia, run!" I tried again.

And this time she must have understood my advice was sound, and joined me in beating a hasty retreat. But even then she found the time to turn around and snap a couple more pictures of the monstrous apparition.

And the weird thing was: the monster seemed eager to pose.

An attention-seeking werewolf. Probably a sign of these social-media-infested times.

We made it to the car, and immediately got in. But before Odelia managed to start her up, the monster was already upon us. It pounced on the car and slammed the hood with its fists, roaring fiercely, and spitting saliva at the windshield like some demon car wash.

"Get us out of here!" Harriet cried frantically.

"It's going to eat us alive!" was Brutus's contribution.

"I don't like this, Max!" were Dooley's two cents.

And me? I just sat there, too stunned for speech.

The monster was crawling on top of the car now, and pouncing on the roof in a clear attempt to punch a hole and drag us out so it could devour us whole.

But then Odelia finally managed to get the engine to turn over, shoved her foot down on the accelerator, and then we were out of there!

There was a thunk and a surprised grunt, and when we looked back we saw the monster lying on the road. As we drove off, it got up and shook its fists at us, raised its formidable fanged maw to the full moon, and roared again— a terrifying sound.

"Victor Ball was right!" Harriet said. "The werewolf exists!"

"And tomorrow morning all of Hampton Cove is going to read my exclusive report and see my exclusive pictures!" said Odelia jubilantly.

She didn't seem to mind one bit we'd almost been mangled to death!

We arrived back at the house and walked in, still trembling from the adrenaline. Harriet immediately made a beeline for her litter box, and as I did the same, I suddenly heard three cries of terror. I immediately walked out of my litter box again, and shot into the backyard, through the hedge and into Marge and Tex's house.

The werewolf!

It had followed us home!

But when I arrived there, I saw that Harriet was shaking, but not with fear and anguish but sheer indignation.

"She did it again! Fifi used my litter box again!"

"She used mine, too!" said Brutus, shaking an irate paw.

"And mine as well," said Dooley sadly.

Marge, Tex and Gran suddenly materialized into the kitchen.

"What's going on?" asked Marge, flicking on the light.

Odelia, who'd run in from next door, along with Chase, now also stood in the kitchen, staring down at four cats, three of which were looking extremely unhappy.

"It's Fifi," I said. "She's been using their litter boxes while we were out."

Then Dooley took a sniff at his litter box, and said, "It wasn't Fifi. It was Rufus."

Odelia closed the kitchen door and looked out, as if expecting Rufus to return for seconds.

Brutus, frowning, sniffed at his litter box. "Well, I'll be damned," he said. "I think it's that dog from down the street. That Cooper something."

We all stared at Harriet, but she shook her head. "Nope. Mine is Fifi, all right. She seems to have selected my litter box for her own."

All eyes turned to Gran, four pairs of cat's eyes included.

"What!" the old lady cried. "So now this is my fault? You're all nuts!"

And with these words, she returned to bed.

"Après moi, le déluge," Tex muttered.

I had no idea what he meant, but it sounded apropos.

*T*he next morning, all of Hampton Cove was atwitter. Odelia's article had appeared in the *Hampton Cove Gazette*, and the phone at the office was ringing off the hook. The picture of the werewolf on the front page had clearly stirred up Odelia's townies, and there was talk of the FBI stepping in, or the army, or even the National Guard.

Odelia's article about the chicken shed had been held back, as both she and Dan felt it needed more work before they dropped that particular bombshell, too.

"I can't believe this," said Dan, shaking his head. He was holding a copy of his own newspaper and staring at the picture of the werewolf.

"Yeah, I found it hard to believe, too," said Odelia, "until I was face to face with the creature."

"No, not the werewolf," said Dan. "Jock! I've known the guy all his life. I stood next to the baptismal font, for crying out loud. And now this."

"Do you think his dad knows?"

"No way. Franklin always treated his animals with kindness and respect. I mean, he was a tough businessman, sure, but he would never allow his chickens to suffer like this."

"I got a call from a guy who works at the chicken plant," said Odelia. "He told me some things you're not going to like, Dan."

"Come on," he said, sitting back. "Give it to me straight."

"The chickens are fed some kind of concoction containing hormones and antibiotics, to make them grow faster, and pack on more meat. It also makes them too sick and too heavy to stand on their feet. And there's more. A lot more."

"God," said Dan. "I have to talk to Jock. I can't just spring this on him. We need to ask him for an official reaction."

Odelia nodded. "Let's publish tomorrow, yeah? We shouldn't sit on this for too long."

She'd been afraid Dan would tell her to drop the story, to protect his friend, but to the editor's credit he'd told her to dig deeper, and by all means pursue the truth, even if it meant exposing Jock.

"I'm starting to wonder now, Dan," said Odelia, deciding to broach another painful topic.

"If a man who can be so cruel to animals could also be cruel to his wife?" asked Dan, anticipating her reflection.

"It's a fair question."

"I know, and it was the first thing that came to mind when you showed me the pictures of those chickens."

"I don't think Grace is buried underneath the chicken shed, though," she said.

"God, Odelia—I hadn't even thought that far!"

"It would be an obvious place to dispose of a body," she argued.

Harriet, Brutus and Dooley had sniffed around the shed, and even though the ammonia and chicken dung had seriously hampered their keen sense of smell, they hadn't picked up anything unusual, and she trusted their judgment implicitly. Whatever happened to Grace and Fabio—they weren't buried underneath that chicken shed.

"Jock told my uncle that he applied for a building permit to erect three or four more of those sheds," she said now. "I think it's important we stop the process of approval in its tracks. It's only going to cause more suffering for those poor animals."

"You're absolutely right. And I'll get on the phone with the Mayor right away. Tell him about the article we're about to publish. Get the proper authorities up to speed."

"I'll drop by the police station," she said, getting up. "I want to know what my uncle plans to do about that werewolf."

Dan smiled. "Now that should be interesting."

It was. When Odelia arrived at the precinct, dozens of people were shouting at the desk sergeant, who wasn't a sergeant at all, but the Mayor's niece Fiona, who clearly wasn't coping well. The girl, who was a strikingly gorgeous and willowy blonde, was red-faced, her blond tresses sticking to the sides of her sweaty face, and trying to control a situation that was quickly spinning out of control.

"I saw it—clear as day!" a woman was shouting. Odelia recognized her as Blanche Captor, a regular at the police station. She was gesticulating wildly, as she described, to anyone who would listen, her encounter with the werewolf. "I'm lucky it didn't kill me!"

Odelia, her curiosity spiked, approached the woman. "Mrs. Captor, where did you see the werewolf exactly?"

"Well, out near Garrison's Field," she said, "close to those woods out there. I was visiting my dear friend Alice Ball— her husband has had another episode and she needed my support, you see. And as I was coming back from the house, and walking to my car, there it was! A monster big as a house! It roared and showed its horrible fangs! And I ran and ran and ran, and when I looked back, it was gone!"

"It didn't attack you?"

"No, it didn't. I guess I was one of the lucky ones."

"Why, has someone been attacked?"

"No, but I heard Scarlett Canyon tripped and fell when she ran from the beast. Nasty cut on her elbow."

"Mh," said Odelia, and walked along to the main open-floor precinct office.

Even there, highly upset citizens were accosting every available police officer, and a harried Alec was trying to drown out their voices by shouting louder than they were.

Finally, he gave up and returned to his office and slammed the door. To no avail. They simply followed him and yanked open his door and crowded around his desk, screaming.

Tough crowd.

She went in search of Chase, and found him next to the coffee machine, where he was smiling before him bemusedly.

"Shouldn't you be out there chasing werewolves?" she asked.

"Oh, that's all taken care of," said Chase. "The Mayor is organizing a volunteer task force. They're going to patrol the area tonight, armed to the teeth no doubt, to catch the beast."

"But... isn't that your job?"

"I thought so, too, but the Mayor decided differently. He said this is a shared responsibility for the whole community, and so the community should handle it."

"What does my uncle think?"

"He's not doing a lot of thinking at the moment," said Chase, taking a sip from his cup of joe. "People are pestering him so much I don't think he's had time to think just yet."

"Fiona isn't coping very well either."

He grinned. "Yeah, I noticed. Too bad, huh? I almost feel sorry for the girl."

"I think you should get a warrant to search Jock Farnsworth's place."

He looked up in surprise. "You think he killed Grace?"

"I do. And I think he hid the body nearby. Either the house or the grounds."

He nodded. "I'll talk to the DA. Get the paperwork started. Alec won't be pleased. He and Jock seem pretty close."

"When he sees the pictures I took of Jock's chicken shed, he'll think differently."

"I know. Who would have thought, huh?"

She'd shown the pictures to Chase last night, and he'd been as horrified as she was. His suggestion had been to bring in animal control, but she felt it was important to compile the full file before alerting Jock to what was going on. Catch him off guard.

"Chase!" Uncle Alec bellowed. "Get in here! Chase!"

Chase gave her a comical grimace. "I guess that's my cue. Watch me go in." And off he went, to save his superior officer from being torn limb from limb by his own citizenry.

Odelia returned to the front desk, and was greeted with a surprising sight: Fiona had picked up her coat and was shouting "I quit! You hear me, you losers?! I quit!" And then she was stalking off towards the exit, presumably with the intention never to return.

And as people howled with indignation, suddenly an irascible voice bellowed, "Silence!"

All eyes turned to the source of the impressive sound.

And there she was: Dolores Peltz, and as she proceeded, parting the masses like a latter-day female Moses, she quickly claimed her rightful position behind the desk.

And as she barked a set of curt orders for people to sit

down and get in line, they all did as they were told, as if moved by an invisible but steely and all-powerful hand.

Odelia smiled, and as she caught Dolores's eye, the older woman gave her a fat wink.

Odelia returned the wink and walked out.

Where would this town be without Dolores? Descending into a welter of chaos, probably.

And then she was heading home.

She'd suddenly had a crazy idea, and decided to put it to the test without delay.

33

---

*W*hen Marge returned to work that morning, she found to her surprise that Jerry and Johnny hadn't arrived yet. The two ex-cons worked long hours, and could usually be found at the library until late at night, trying to finish that wonky old wall for her.

They were really devoted to their work, that much was obvious.

When she stepped behind her desk, she found a brown paper envelope sticking up between the keys of her keyboard. On it, the words 'For Marge' had been written in a spidery scrawl she recognized as Johnny's.

She opened the envelope, only to find a contract inside. It appeared to have been drawn up a couple of weeks before, and the only name that jumped out at her was the Mayor's, Dirk Dunham.

What was one of the Mayor's contracts doing on her desk?

And suddenly a feeling of apprehension took hold of her, and she quickly headed for the stairs that led into the basement. And even before she'd reached the back wall where the two ex-cons had done such a great job, she had a feeling she knew what she'd find.

A blue plastic tarp had been placed in front of the wall, and she pulled it aside. She now remembered she hadn't seen that wall since the day the reformed crooks had started work.

She wasn't surprised, therefore, to find behind it a tunnel gaping back at her.

"Oh, Johnny," she murmured, and took a flashlight that had conveniently been left behind by the twosome, and switched it on. Heading deeper into the tunnel, she had to admire the fine craftsmanship that had gone into its creation: it was easily a hundred feet long, and was supported with jagged pieces of metal that looked as if they'd been swiped from a local scrapyard. Finally, she arrived at a steel wall, where several holes had been cut with a blowtorch, which was still lying in evidence at her feet.

And even as she stared into one of the holes, a little door on the other side was opened and she found herself staring into the stupefied face of her neighbor: bank manager Brady Dexter.

&.

"*I* have another mission for you!" said Odelia the moment she stepped through the door.

We'd been lounging on the couch, taking repose and getting our strength back after the hair-raising events of the night before. I felt we deserved this little break. But now it was apparently over already.

"What mission?" asked Brutus, perking up.

Brutus has never been one for lounging about for interminable lengths of time. He's an action cat, and inactivity saps his strength.

"I would like you to pay another visit to the Farnsworth place, and this time I want you to use your noses."

"Our noses?" I asked, mystified.

"I have reason to believe Grace's body has been buried somewhere inside that house, or the grounds surrounding it, and I want you to prove that you can sniff out a dead body as well as a dog can."

"Oh, don't you doubt it," said Harriet, who was still sore about the litter box incident, and now harbored a particular grudge against all dogs, great or small.

"So prove it," said Odelia with a smile as she offered up this challenge.

"Prove what?" asked Dooley, who'd just entered the kitchen through the pet flap.

"We're going to find a dead body," I said, getting him up to speed on the latest events.

"A dead body?" he asked. "Did the werewolf kill someone?"

"Not the werewolf. Jock Farnsworth," said Odelia.

"Oh, him," said Dooley, losing his interest. The werewolf encounter had set him thinking, and he seemed to consider the monster a friend rather than a foe. In fact he'd told us he wouldn't mind another face-to-face meeting, and this time he'd engage it in conversation. Try to find out what made it tick.

I'd told him what made it tick was an intense desire for blood and guts, but he said it probably was just a creature like the rest of us, yearning for some love and affection.

Brutus had told him he was nuts, and that had been the end of that conversation.

"Let's go," said Odelia, who didn't believe in wasting time.

So we went out the door, into her pickup, and then we were on our way, making good time as she headed out of town, even as people all seemed eager to get into town, as proven by the long line of traffic going the other direction.

"All going to the police station no doubt," said Odelia. "You should have seen them. Practically mobbing my uncle."

"People are scared," I said. "And they have every reason to be."

"Yeah, I was scared, too," said Harriet. "Though I'm more scared of Fifi taking another dump in my litter box while we're gone."

"I told her not to," I said. "But I don't think she was paying attention."

"She invited all the dogs of the neighborhood to use our litter boxes," said Harriet sadly. "She's decided to be the best ambassador she can be of the litter revolution, and when I told her the litter revolution is a bust, she said she understood. It often happens that the original founders of a movement step back, only for the second generation to take over. And now it's happening to the litter movement, and she's happy to take over."

"I'll talk to Kurt," said Odelia. "Make him buy Fifi a litter box. I'll even pay him."

"Or fix that hole in the fence," said Brutus. "That seems to be the way they all get in."

"Or I could temporarily block the pet door," said Odelia, but that only drew horrified cries from the four of us. "Okay," she said with a laugh. "I guess not. But I will make sure to always close the kitchen door from now on."

We'd arrived at the entrance to the Farnsworth domain and she parked the car.

"Okay, this is it, you guys. I'll ring the bell, and you slip in through the back, all right? Are you ready to do this?"

"We're ready," I said determinedly.

"Are we going to meet the werewolf after this?" asked

Dooley. "I think I know what I'm going to say to him. I've prepared a speech."

"No, Dooley," said Odelia. "We're not going to meet the werewolf. Besides, werewolves only come out at night, when the moon is full."

"So where is he now?" asked Dooley, visibly disappointed.

"He's in his human form," said Harriet.

"Yeah, probably working as a bank teller or an insurance broker or a trash collector," said Brutus. "It's always the ones you least expect it from."

"Okay, this is it," said Odelia, who clearly felt it was time for action. "Let's go!"

34

*F*ather Reilly had been lighting a few candles in his church, and was just staring down at his nice tile floor, wondering how many layers of dog dung had been stamped into it, and whether he should contract a deep cleaning service, when Victor Ball walked in.

"Oh, hi, Victor," he said. "What a nice surprise. What brings you here?"

Victor glanced around a little uncertainly, his mustache quivering gently.

"Um... you told me to join your meeting, so..." He spread his arms and gave a sheepish little grin. "Here I am."

"I also told you the meeting is Monday nights at eight, and what day is today, Victor?"

If he disliked being treated like a five-year-old, Victor didn't show it. Instead, he thought hard. "Um... Thursday?"

"Come back on Monday, and you'll find a group of the warmest, most inviting people you could ever hope to meet."

But Victor didn't budge. Instead, he just stood there, now tugging at his mustache as if hoping it would give him strength.

Father Reilly, who was a patient man, and a people person, saw that here was a person in need, and so he walked over and put a hand on the man's shoulder. "I can see there's something on your mind, Victor. Out with it. Come on."

When the man still appeared hesitant, the priest said, "Would you feel more comfortable if we take this into the confession booth?"

"I would, yes," said Victor finally, and with a sweeping gesture, Father Reilly led this troubled soul into the small booth.

The moment they were both comfortably seated, Father Reilly opened the hatch, and said, "What is it, Victor? You know you can unburden your soul with only the Lord as your witness, and that nothing you say goes beyond this confessional."

"Yes, father," said Victor dutifully.

"How long has it been since your last confession?"

"Too long, father."

"Well, then. No time like the present. What's preying on your mind, son?"

"The thing is, Father, I'm at a quandary."

Father Reilly, surprised that Victor would be familiar with such a big word, hid his astonishment well. All he said was, "Oh?"

"I had an offer that's too good to refuse, father, but Alice told me to say no, so I did say no, but then I said yes, and now I don't know what to tell Alice."

"And what offer would that be?" asked the priest, pretty sure it involved the services of some wanton woman at one of the bars in town Victor liked to frequent.

"It's the Mayor, see. He's offered to buy my property, and he's offered a fine price for it, too. But Alice says over her dead body will she ever sell the house where generations of Balls have been raised. She told me to tell the Mayor to go to hell, and so I did tell him to go to hell, and he didn't take it well."

"Mayor Dunham wants to buy your property? What does he intend to do with it?"

He couldn't imagine what Mayor Dunham would want with a dilapidated old farmhouse and the surrounding bit of barren land located in the middle of the woods.

"I don't know, father, but Giles down the road got the same offer, and he's also refusing to sell, and I heard there are more farmers told to sell up. Some of them did, some of them didn't."

"Huh," said the priest. "And so what's your quandary, son? You feel bad about telling the Mayor to go to hell, is that it?"

He would tell the Mayor to go to hell in a heartbeat. He didn't like his bullying ways, and he certainly didn't like that he was trying to get his good friend Chief Alec to take early retirement.

"No, father. It's just that... The Mayor then upped his offer, complimenting me on driving such a hard bargain, and the second time I actually told him I'd accept, and so he already paid me an advance. In cash. And I'm pretty sure Alice is going to be pretty mad."

"I think you owe it to Alice to tell her the truth, Victor."

"But the thing is, father, that Alice is very fond of her rolling pin. She likes to use it on my head, and I have a feeling if I tell her I sold the house she's going to do a lot more than beat the living shit out of me. She's going to go berserk and use my head like a drum. She loves that house, even more than I do, and was real adamant about not selling."

"So what made you go behind her back?"

"It was a big fat advance the Mayor gave me, father."

"So maybe you can give it back? Explain to the Mayor

how you changed your mind. No contracts were signed, right? This was merely a verbal agreement?"

"See, the thing is—I more or less spent the money, father. So there's nothing to give back."

"Oh, dear."

"It's a quandary, father," said Victor. "A genuine quandary."

"It certainly is," he agreed. "How much did the Mayor give you?"

"Ten thousand dollars."

"Ten thou— and you spent it?" He didn't need to ask what Victor spent the money on. That was quite obvious. "You know what we'll do? I'll have a talk with Alice, and I'm going to explain to her what happened, and I'm going to advise her against the use of her rolling pin for any purpose other than the preparation of her fine bread and pastry. How does that sound to you? And perhaps I can have a word with the Mayor, too. Tell him about your predicament, and ask if you can't pay him back the money in installments."

"Oh, would you, father? Would you really?"

"It's the least I can do for a member of my flock," said the priest warmly.

Victor was clearly much relieved. In fact he was over the moon. "Thank you, Father Reilly. Thank you so much. That would be a big help. Alice would never hit a priest."

"Why don't I drop by the house later and you and Alice and I sit down for that chat?"

It was perhaps too much to say that Victor walked out of the church with a spring in his step, as a man who's been drinking as much as he had for as long as he had has a hard time walking straight, even when sober, but a weight had clearly been lifted from his shoulders. And as Father Reilly watched him leave, he found his mind wandering back to the man's words. Why did the Mayor want to buy up a bunch of old farmhouses and surrounding land? What was he planning to do with them?

And then, vowing to get to the bottom of this thing, he took out his phone and called the woman he'd come to consider an ally.

"Vesta? Do you have a minute?"

So far everything had gone according to plan. Odelia had rung the front doorbell, while the rest of us snuck in through the kitchen door.

Once we were inside, we split up in two teams, and used our noses to discover whether Grace and Fabio's bodies might have been buried somewhere on the premises. Once we'd gone over the house, we'd meet back in the kitchen, and cover the grounds.

It was a gruesome task, of course, and frankly I wasn't exactly looking forward to it. I've never been much of a cadaver dog, or even a cadaver cat, but Odelia said it needed to be done, so do it we did.

"Let's start in the basement," I suggested.

"Why is it that people always hide dead bodies in the basement, Max?" asked Dooley. "Why can't they hide them in the bathroom or the bedroom instead?"

"Because people don't like to take a shower next to a dead body," I said, "or sleep next to one. Out of sight, out of mind, and what better place to get rid of a dead body than to bury it under a nice slab of concrete in the basement where no one will ever find it?"

"I guess so," he said, still not fully convinced. Which just goes to show Dooley would make a lousy murderer.

We carefully made our way down a set of stone steps into the Farnsworth basement, and found a nice collection of wines and spirits all neatly organized on wooden racks.

"Looks like Jock is an alcoholic," said Dooley.

"It's not because people enjoy a glass of wine now and then that they're necessarily alcoholics, Dooley," I said. "Odelia and Chase like the occasional glass of wine with their dinner, and so do Marge and Tex. That doesn't make them raging alcoholics."

"It doesn't?"

"There's a difference between enjoying a sip of wine and drinking it by the gallon," I intimated as I let my eyes drift past the rows and rows of wine, all displayed labels out, and then resumed my task of sniffing around for traces of dead bodies. But as far as I could tell the only dead bodies located there were cockroaches, beetles, rats and mice.

And as we headed deeper into the basement, it soon became clear that wherever Jock had stashed his wife and her lover, it wasn't down there.

"Too bad," Dooley said. "I think Odelia is really looking forward to finding Grace."

"She's looking forward to finding her alive," I corrected him. "And hopefully she is."

We climbed those stairs again, and when we reached the kitchen Harriet and Brutus had just returned from their search of the rest of the house.

"And? Find anything?" asked Harriet hopefully.

"Nothing," I said.

"Lots of wine," said Dooley.

177

We could hear Odelia's voice. She was talking to Jock, keeping him distracted while her cats inspected his property.

"Let's check those grounds," I said.

This was a much tougher proposition, as they were really stretched out, and Grace and Fabio could be buried anywhere.

Still, I trusted that our keen senses of smell would carry us through and save the day.

So we headed outside, and as Harriet and Brutus turned left, Dooley and I turned right. We'd circle around and meet back by Odelia's car.

Dooley and I kept our noses close to the ground, as we sniffed around. We're not as well-versed in sniffing out bodies as dogs, perhaps, but we're no amateurs either. And soon I thought I'd picked up what smelled like Grace. Odelia had handed us a dress that had belonged to her, so we could pick up her scent, and I now thought I was onto something. Dooley had smelled it, too, for he said, "I think I've got something, Max."

Our search led us in the direction of a remote part of the domain, and we were actually not all that far from the chicken shed now. A derelict smaller shed that had weathered many a storm, nevertheless still stood erect. We were on a hill, and could see the chicken shed and the farm from where we sat, and had a good view of the house, too.

"I never noticed this shed before," said Dooley as we stared at the crooked structure.

"Me neither," I said. "I guess we missed it when we passed here yesterday."

We moved closer, and saw that the door was locked. The wood was decayed in places, though, and we managed to enter through an opening between two wooden planks.

Once inside, it took us a moment for our eyes to adjust.

The scent of Grace had become much stronger, and there was a second scent mixed in with the first. Could it be Fabio?

And then suddenly I saw it: two people sat there, trussed up nice and good.

"I think we found them, Dooley," I said.

"Are they dead?" he asked.

"I don't know. Let's find out, shall we?"

We moved a little closer, and I immediately sensed body heat. I'm not an expert, but dead people tend to be cold to the touch, so it was obvious these two were still alive.

Just then, I could hear footsteps approaching, and the two trussed-up figures started moving and hollering something I couldn't understand as they had gags in their mouths.

There was a rattle of chains, and I said, "Quick, Dooley. Hide!"

And quick as a flash—or two flashes—we hid behind an old cupboard in a corner of the small space.

A shaft of light fell on us when the door was opened a crack, then opened further.

A man stepped inside, and I immediately recognized him as the same man who'd chased us from the chicken shed the night before.

"It's the same man!" Dooley said, excitedly.

"Shush, Dooley," I said.

I didn't want to suffer the same fate as Grace and Fabio, who clearly had become the man's prisoners for some reason.

The man removed the gags, then placed a Tupperware container on the table and removed the lid. The scent of something edible wafted in my direction, and I recognized it as broccoli, eggs and potatoes. Not exactly the most sumptuous meal for a person like Grace Farnsworth, probably more accustomed to dining at five-star restaurants.

Grace said, "You have to let us go, Gino. You can't keep us here forever."

But Gino didn't respond.

"Do you hear me? Tell my husband he can't do this. When the police find out what he's been up to, there will be hell to pay, and that goes for you, too."

"Oh, shut up already, will you?" growled the man.

"This is an outrage," said Fabio. "I'll complain to my manager about this. Nowhere did it say in my contract that I would be subjected to this kind of horrible treatment!"

"And you shut up as well, painter boy," said the man. "Now eat."

He'd released the prisoners' ties so they could eat, and they did so now, with visible and audible relish. I guess everything tastes better when you're hungry. Meanwhile, the man kept a close eye on them, making sure they didn't escape. I saw he was casually holding a gun, which he loosely pointed in their direction.

"How much longer are you going to keep us here?" asked Grace.

The man shrugged. "As long as the boss tells me to."

"And how long will that be?" she insisted.

"Enough with the questions. Shut up and eat."

"We have to tell Odelia," I whispered.

"I can't believe Jock would lock up his own wife!" said Dooley.

Unfortunately our meowing, even though hushed, had attracted the man's attention. He stomped his rubber-booted foot, shouting, "Get out of here, you filthy cats! Now get!"

And get we did, fleeing swiftly, then racing back to the house to meet Odelia and give her the good news.

Grace and Fabio were still alive. The less than good news was that the man who could have been Odelia's dad in a different life was a criminal.

36

"So I'm afraid we're nowhere closer to finding out what happened to your wife, Mr. Farnsworth," Odelia said.

"Well, thank you for driving all the way out here to keep me informed," said Jock courteously. "And I'm sorry Alicia couldn't be here. But I'll be sure to tell her."

"You haven't heard from your wife by any chance?"

"No, not a single word, I'm afraid," said the man, looking as dapper and handsome as ever. His gray hair was perfectly coiffed, his polo shirt neatly ironed. There was even a crease in his pants.

"The thing is, my uncle is pretty swamped with this were-wolf story," said Odelia.

"Ah, yes, the werewolf. Interesting story. You met the beast yourself?"

"I did, yes. I would never have believed the stories if I hadn't seen it with my own two eyes."

"So it's true? There is a monster out there?"

"I'm afraid so. I met it near Garrison's Field last night."

Jock nodded. "I saw the pictures you took. Hard to believe

such a creature could actually exist, and have kept out of sight for all these years. Though of course there have been rumors. Farmers whose sheep have been killed, cows attacked in the middle of the night. We always assumed wolves were responsible. I myself have had chickens slaughtered, which I attributed to foxes. But I would never have thought a werewolf..."

"Yes, it's hard to imagine," she agreed, wondering if she'd given Max and Dooley and the others enough time now to conduct a thorough search of the house.

"Still, the pictures speak for themselves. Your uncle will probably organize a search party to hunt the beast down?"

"Actually the Mayor is organizing a group of volunteers tonight, to search those fields and surrounding woods."

"Well done. Mayor Dunham is really taking control of the situation."

"He is," said Odelia. "I guess he wants the beast caught before these stories and sightings start to affect the tourist trade."

"Of course," said Jock, nodding. "So how is Marge? I must say it was wonderful seeing her again after all those years. I've seen her in town in passing, but never had the chance to talk to her until yesterday."

"She's fine," said Odelia.

"Good. Good."

The conversation was a little strained and stilted, which Odelia attributed to her desire to drag it out as long as she could, to give Max and the others the opportunity to search the house undetected. But there was also something about the man she couldn't quite put her finger on. He was friendly enough, but she still got the sense he was hiding something. Of course she was, too. Not just about the fact that she was about to expose his chicken operation, but also the suspicions she harbored that he was responsible for whatever had happened to this wife.

But he couldn't possibly know that, could he?

He'd gotten up and swiftly moved over to the door. Then, much to her surprise, closed the door and turned the key in the lock. She couldn't believe her eyes.

His charming smile remained firmly in place, but had acquired a menacing quality.

"You haven't exactly been forthcoming with me, have you, Odelia?"

"What do you mean?" she asked, her heart having skipped a beat. Was she in danger? Was he going to kill her like he'd killed his wife?

"Mayor Dunham called me just before you arrived. He told me about your visit to my farm last night. And my foreman Gino Nickel told me this morning we'd had nocturnal visitors. Of course I couldn't have imagined it was you, but there it is."

"Mayor Dunham told you, but how?"

"Your editor called him this morning, to formally ask him to launch an investigation into my business practices. Animal cruelty was mentioned, and animal control."

"And instead of calling animal control, the Mayor called you."

"Oh, Dirk Dunham and I go way back," said Jock now, as he took a seat.

"You can't keep me here, Jock," she said. "Dan knows where I am, and so does Chase."

"I have no intention of keeping you here, Odelia. I just want to explain a few things to you. When my father handed me the business several years ago, we were on the verge of bankruptcy. You see, it's very difficult to make a profit as a small-time chicken farmer these days. You need to scale up, while still keeping down your costs, which is impossible without, shall we say, cutting a few corners."

"By treating your animals like chattel, you mean," she said, the images of those poor animals still burned on her retinae.

"I treat my animals fairly well, compared to some of my colleagues. Of course, the old story of chickens clucking happily away while they scurry round the barnyard is long gone. That isn't an economically viable model. So you see, it's not as if I have a choice here. It's either this, or no chicken business in Hampton Cove at all. And Dirk Dunham, being an economic realist, and not a dreamer like some of these animal rights activists, knows this, and has supported my vision for the future of Hampton Cove from the first. Now all I want to ask you is to reconsider publishing that article."

"I'm publishing my article, Jock, and the pictures that go with it," she said.

He got up, his jaw working. "I guess I expected more from Marge's daughter."

"I can't turn a blind eye to animal cruelty. And if you can't run a chicken business without torturing those poor animals, maybe you shouldn't be in the chicken business."

"I think we're done here," he said, and walked to the door, and unlocked it.

She walked out, her heart still beating a mile a minute, and her throat dry.

"You're not getting away with this, you know," he said as she walked past him.

"No, it's you who isn't getting away with this," she said, and stalked along the corridor until she'd reached the front door.

She expected him to stop her, but when she looked back he was nowhere to be found.

She walked out and closed the door behind her, then hurried back to her car.

Max, Dooley, Brutus and Harriet were waiting for her, seated on the hood of the car.

"We found Grace and Fabio," said Max. "They're locked up in a shed near the chicken farm. And they're alive and well. Apart from the broccoli they're forced to eat, of course."

37

*C*hase didn't know where to look first. The precinct was being overrun by concerned citizens inquiring after the werewolf sightings. As it turned out, very few people had actually seen the beast. Most had just read Odelia's article and seen the pictures.

By the time Chase and his fellow officers had managed to calm down the frantic citizenry besieging the police station, Odelia's call came in.

"We found Grace and Fabio. Jock locked them up in an old shed near his farm."

"Don't do anything. I'll be there in five," he promised, and then relayed the message to Chief Alec, who decided to drop everything and join him.

"I can't believe Jock would do such a thing," said the Chief as they raced through Hampton Cove, their police siren whining away and the light flashing on the roof.

"Yeah, I don't understand the reasoning," said Chase. "Why lock up Grace?"

"To punish her because she was unfaithful? But wouldn't she go to the police the first chance she got?"

"Let's hear what he has to say—but first we need to free her and Fabio."

They arrived at Jock's house in next to no time where Odelia was already waiting.

Chase and Alec walked up to the front door and rang the bell, and when Jock opened the door, looking mystified, Chase said, "We have reason to believe your wife is being held prisoner on your property, sir. We could either arrange for a warrant or—"

"No, that's all right," said Jock, a concerned look on his face. He stepped out and closed the door behind him. "By all means, let's find her. Where is she being held?"

"I don't know—Odelia found her," said Chief Alec.

He cut an accusing look in Odelia's direction. "She did, did she? She didn't mention that to me when she visited me earlier."

"I think that's because she figures *you* put your wife there," said Chase.

"Me? Lock up Grace?" He laughed an incredulous laugh. "That's ridiculous!"

"Who else could have done it? It's your property," said Odelia, not too kindly.

"You have the wrong idea about me," said Jock, shaking his head. "I would never do anything to hurt Grace. Never."

They had walked the short distance to the shed, Odelia leading the way. When they arrived, Chase saw that the door was unlocked, a chain dangling from it.

He carefully opened the door and looked inside.

The shed was empty.

"Did you find her?" Jock called out. "Is she in there?"

"Empty," said Chase as Odelia appeared next to him.

"But... I don't understand," she said. "They were in here half an hour ago."

"Did you see them?"

"No, Max and Dooley did, and they wouldn't lie about something like this."

"Whoever kept them here must have smelled a rat and moved them," said Chase.

"Where is my wife?" asked Jock, now also entering the small shed. He glanced around. "Where is she?"

"Oh, don't you play dumb with me," said Odelia. "You had them moved, didn't you?"

"What, me? Of course not! You have to believe me—I had nothing to do with this. So you saw them in here? With your own eyes?"

Odelia hesitated, and Chase said, "They were here half an hour ago, so they can't be far."

His eyes fell on the chicken house. "Let's take a look over there."

The small company set foot for the chicken house, Chief Alec sputtering something about his feet as they climbed down from the hill and he stubbed his toe on a rock.

Behind them, four cats had fallen in line with the four humans making their way down, and Chase could hear Max say something to Odelia that he didn't understand.

Jock glanced over, and frowned at the cats. "Where did they come from?"

"They're my cats," said Odelia, "and they have an excellent sense of smell. If Grace and Fabio are around here somewhere, you can bet they'll find them."

"I hope you're right," said Jock. "And if I find whoever has been holding my wife..."

They'd arrived at the large chicken house, and Jock pushed open the heavy sliding door. Inside, chickens were roaming around, clucking happily and picking at seed being dispensed with a generous hand by one of Jock's workers.

"But..." said Odelia, visibly surprised. "There were a lot more chickens in here last night."

"Ah, yes," said Jock. "I had temporarily housed some more animals in here, while a second shed was under construction. Luckily it was finally finished and so we moved some of the chickens into the new shed. Now they have plenty of space, they can even roam around outside if they like. Everything perfectly up to code and according to regulations, as you can see." He waved to the man dispensing the feed. "Everything all right, Gino?"

"Chickens happy as clams, sir," said the man, waving a hand.

"I like to see my chickens happy," said Jock. "Happy chickens make me happy, too."

"You tricked me!" said Odelia, accosting the chicken wing king.

"Tricked you? What do you mean?" asked Jock, confused.

Chase glanced around. Obviously these chickens were being raised in excellent circumstances, and any animal control inspectors would have nothing to cavil at.

"Let's find Grace and Fabio," he said now.

"Can I have a word with you in private, Detective?" asked Jock.

They walked out of the shed, and Jock glanced back, a look of concern on his face. "It's Odelia," he said. "I'm worried about her. She barged in earlier, accusing me of mistreating my chickens, while you can see for yourself her accusations are unfounded. Then she accused me of kidnapping my wife and keeping her locked up in that shed, while there is no sign of Grace. I think seeing that werewolf last night—or whatever that creature was—must have brought on some sort of traumatic episode, causing her to act out now."

But Chase wasn't having any of this nonsense. "I saw the pictures myself, Jock. Last night this shed was overloaded with chickens, living cheek to jowl. I don't know who

189

warned you off, but someone clearly did. And as far as your wife is concerned, if Odelia says she saw them in that shed, she saw them in that shed. I don't know what game you think you're playing here, but it's not going to work."

Jock gave him a look of shock. "Detective! You're not honestly accusing me of... Alec! Listen to this. Your detective is actually thinking I had something to do with my wife's disappearance. He can't be serious, right?"

But Alec held up his hands. "I don't know what's going on here, Jock, but it stinks."

Chase sniffed. It certainly did.

3 8

*O*delia was taking a proverbial beating. First Grace and Fabio had disappeared. Again. And now the chickens had suddenly been redistributed. Obviously Jock had been given a heads-up about Odelia's investigation, and had taken precautions.

"Are you sure you saw them?" asked Harriet.

"Yes, we saw them," I said. "Both Grace and Fabio were being held in that shed."

We all stared up at the hill where the shed was located. The door was open now, and nothing indicated anyone had ever been locked up in there.

"I don't understand," said Dooley. "How can they suddenly disappear?"

"Maybe you saw a mirage," said Brutus. "It happens. You think you see something, and in actual fact it's not there at all. Like an oasis in the desert."

"No, we saw them," I insisted. I couldn't believe my keen eyesight was being questioned by my fellow cats.

"Did you really see them?" asked Odelia now, crouching down next to us.

191

"Yes, we saw them!" I said. "They were there."

Odelia studied me thoughtfully. A little ways away Jock stood talking to Uncle Alec and Chase. Clearly the investigation had hit a snag, in the form of the missing abductees. And the chickens suddenly being treated humanely didn't help Odelia's case either.

She'd risen to her feet and stood, hands on hips, thinking hard.

"Let's get out of here," her uncle said now. "Nothing to see."

"If we don't find them now, we never will," I said. "Jock will make them disappear for sure. And this time permanently. He can't risk them being found. Not after this."

Odelia nodded, to indicate she'd heard me.

"I don't smell anything," said Brutus, sniffing the air. "All I smell is chickens. Lots and lots of chickens."

I wandered over in the direction of the chicken shed, and a plump chicken came waddling up to me. I recognized her as the chicken we'd had such a nice chat with the night before.

"Thank you, cat," she said. "Our circumstances have improved considerably since your intervention."

"I didn't do anything," I said. "Jock is simply covering his tracks now that he's under investigation."

"Whatever you did or didn't do, we're all grateful," she said. "So thank you, cat."

"Max," I said. "My name is Max."

"You can call me Bertha," she said.

"I thought you didn't have a name?"

She smiled. "I've decided to adopt one from now on."

"Bertha. I like it," I said. "It suits you." And then I thought of something. "Did you by any chance see a man and a woman being taken out of that shed on that hill over there?"

"You mean Grace? Oh, sure. She and her friend were taken into that trailer just now."

"They were? What trailer?"

"The yellow one over there—the big one. It's been there ever since they started construction on the second shed."

"Thank you so much, Bertha," I said. "I owe you one."

"No, you don't. I owed you one."

I hurried back, and was just in time to see Chase, Alec, Jock and Odelia walk up the hill, in the direction of the main house.

"Wait!" I yelled. "I know where he's keeping Grace!"

Odelia turned back, and said, "Wait up, Uncle Alec."

"What is it now?" asked Jock, clearly annoyed.

"She's in that trailer over there," I said.

Odelia stared at the trailer, a glint of hope in her eyes.

"And yes, I'm sure. Bertha saw her—one of the chickens."

"I want that trailer checked," said Odelia now, pointing to the trailer.

"Not again," said Jock. "Can't you see she's delusional? I mean, I'm sorry to have to tell you this, Alec, but clearly your niece is losing it—no offense."

Alec hesitated.

"And may I remind you that you're my guests?" Jock added. "I don't want to play hardball here, but you don't even have a warrant. So technically I could ask you to leave."

"Do you want to find your wife or not, Jock?" said Chase.

"Of course I want to find my wife! But you're not going to find her in a trailer!"

"Grace!" Odelia called out. "Grace, are you there?"

"Oh, please," said Jock. "This is embarrassing. Please, for her own sake, stop your niece, Alec."

"Odelia, honey," said Alec. "Maybe it's time to head on home now."

"Grace!" Odelia bellowed, now running towards the trailer. Suddenly the door opened and Gino walked out.

When he saw Odelia racing towards him, he directed a look of uncertainty at Jock.

"Stop her, Gino! She's completely lost it!"

"Um, miss. You're not supposed to be here," he said, holding up his hand like a traffic cop.

But Odelia wasn't deterred. "Grace!"

"Stop her, for crying out loud! Can't you see she's deranged?!"

Odelia had now entered the trailer, and we all waited with bated breath. Had Bertha made a bloomer? Had I?

And then, suddenly, Odelia reappeared, a look of satisfaction on her face. Behind her, Grace walked out, looking much the worse for wear, and then, finally, Fabio.

"Jock, you bastard!" Grace yelled.

And then Jock was running up that hill.

"Oh, you've got to be kidding me," said Uncle Alec, but lucky for him he had a fit and healthy deputy, and within seconds Chase was in hot pursuit.

We watched on as Jock clambered up the hill, but even before he reached the summit, Chase was upon him, and grabbed his legs. Both men fell and came tumbling down. At the bottom, a puddle of chicken dung was waiting, and they now both plunged into it.

"Yuck," said Harriet. "That's going to smell."

Jock wasn't giving in, though, and put up a good fight. The men exchanged a few blows, then fell down again. By then they were both covered in mud and chicken muck from head to toe, and were grappling like a pair of wannabe pro wrestlers.

Finally Chase got the upper hand and managed to subdue the chicken wing king, who cried out, "You can't do this! I didn't do anything!"

"You locked me up in a frickin shed, Jock!" Grace yelled. "Who does that?"

"I'm lodging a formal complaint with the painters' association," said Fabio. "And I can you tell right now they are not to be trifled with."

Chase dragged the other man to his feet and came trudging out of that puddle. "Handcuffs, Alec," he said, panting.

"Use your own," said Alec. "I'm not giving you my nice and shiny handcuffs. You'll only get them dirty."

"Oh, just give him the handcuffs, Uncle Alec," said Odelia.

And so Alec did as he was told. In due time Jock was handcuffed and read his rights while Alec called in reinforcements.

"I owe you an apology, Max," said Harriet. "I thought you and Dooley had imagined things, but clearly you hadn't."

"I guess it wasn't an oasis in the desert," said Brutus, eyeing Chase with distaste.

"Jock knows about you guys," said Odelia now. "He must have heard the rumors about me and my cats, and when this Gino Nickel guy told him he saw you in that shed up there, he must have figured better safe than sorry, and had Grace and Fabio moved."

"Well, now he's the one being locked up," I said. "And good riddance, too."

"He's a smooth operator," said Odelia. "He's such a skilled liar I was actually starting to doubt myself."

"Good thing Marge never married him," said Harriet. "Or else he'd be your dad."

"Oh, God forbid," said Odelia with a slight shiver.

Alec had placed Gino Nickel under arrest, and both him and Jock now sat gloomily waiting to be taken to the police station.

"You did great, Odelia," said Alec now. "And I'm getting

animal control out here ASAP. I'm pretty sure there's about a ton of regulations Jock has been violating." Just then, his phone dinged, and he picked up. "Yes, Marge," he said good-naturedly. He listened for a moment, then his face sagged. "The bank? Robbed? You've got to be kidding me!"

$\mathcal{M}$ ayor Dirk Dunham was in his office, staring out the window. Down below, Hampton Cove stretched out before him. His town. His dominion. He smiled as he watched Hampton Covians walk past Town Hall, going about their business, while their beloved Mayor watched on, guarding over them like a benevolent god—all-knowing, all-seeing.

He liked the feeling. He liked being in control, and as he contemplated expanding his vision to include not just Hampton Cove but perhaps the entire county, or even the state, his thoughts returned to some troubling events that had transpired that morning.

Jock had called, telling him that nosy reporter Odelia Poole had been snooping around his chicken farm last night. At least he thought it was her, for no other reporter would be accompanied by a small contingent of cats. He had been able to confirm that it had, indeed, been the Poole woman, as her editor had called in to tell him they were running an article on the chicken farm and he should probably call animal control.

That was the advantage of having friends in many places. Friends like Dan Goory, or even Chase Kingsley, Hampton Cove's next chief of police. Chase would be able to keep that nosy parker girlfriend of his on a tight leash, and so would her editor Dan.

He looked up with a touch of annoyance when his secretary walked in, and announced that his niece was there to see him.

"Send her in," he growled. Fiona was a sweet girl, and he had big plans for her, but she was also one of those high-maintenance women who needed a lot of attention. He hated high-maintenance women, or giving his attention where it wasn't due.

"Fiona, darling, how nice to see you," he said, his frown easily morphing into a smile.

Her face was a thundercloud, though. She clearly wasn't her usual radiant self.

"I quit that lousy job you gave me, Uncle Dirk. I hate it. Hate it!"

She was in foot-stomping mood. "You quit the police station job? But why?"

"People kept pestering me about that stupid werewolf. It was horrible. They were badgering me and harassing me and I just lost it. So I told them I quit—and I did!"

"That's all right, darling. You don't have to do anything you don't like."

"I know. So now what do I do?"

"Um… You could help out here in Town Hall? Join my administration?"

"You know I hate typing, Uncle Dirk. Don't you have a fun job instead?"

"Sure, um…" He thought hard. "Something fun… like what?"

"Well, I could oversee the construction of the new town hall. That would be fun."

He'd been planning to raze the old town hall to the ground and erect a completely new building, state-of-the-art, with an entire floor devoted to himself and his legacy.

"But you don't know the first thing about construction, honey, or architecture."

She waved an airy hand. "I'll learn on the job. How hard can it be?"

"Well…"

The door opened again, and this time Vesta Muffin came charging in. "I know what you're up to and I won't stand for it!" she announced.

"Oh, get lost, you horrible woman," said Fiona, but Dirk silenced her with a gesture. "What can I do for you, Vesta?" he asked, always remembering these people were his voters, and he needed to appease them.

"You're trying to buy up all the land south of Garrison's Field. What are you up to? Huh? I'll bet it's nothing good!"

He laughed what he hoped was a careless laugh. "I don't know what you're talking about, Vesta. Honestly I don't."

"Victor Ball said you bought up his land, and several of his neighbors. So what's your game, huh? A new shopping mall? Housing tract? Factory? Spill, you spineless weasel!"

"Uncle Dirk, do you want me to throw her out?" asked Fiona. "Cause I will."

But before he could respond, the door flew open again, and Marge Poole walked in, waving some kind of document.

"I know what you're up to, Dirk. You and Jock Farnsworth and Jerome Winkle! You're rezoning the land around Garrison's Field as an industrial zone, aren't you? Destroy all those nice woods and get rid of all of those small farms and turn them into factories! You can't do that—it's illegal!"

"Um... I'm sure I don't know what you're talking about, Marge," he said, starting to feel a little hot under his collar all of a sudden.

"I have it all right here," she said, slapping the document down on his desk. "It's the contract you signed with Jock and Jerome to rezone the entire area, probably netting you millions in the process."

"How did you get this?" he asked as he picked up the contract. "It was in my safe."

"Your safe was broken into last night, I'm not sorry to say, as well as half a dozen other safes."

"Oh, my God!" said Dirk, horrified. This was a disaster!

The door flew open again, and Brady Dexter barged in. "I'm so sorry, Mr. Mayor," the bank manager said, visibly distraught, "but I'm afraid the bank was burgled last night. Criminals got into half a dozen safes, one of which was yours, unfortunately. They've absconded with their entire contents. I thought I'd tell you personally."

Dirk sank down onto his chair. This wasn't happening.

"Do you want me to throw all these people out, uncle?" asked Fiona. "I don't mind."

Dirk didn't respond, but merely stared at the door, half expecting it to fly open again, and then it did!

Alec Lip came barging in, followed by Chase Kingsley and Odelia Poole.

"You're under arrest, Dirk Dunlap," said the Chief, "for aiding and abetting the kidnapping and false imprisonment of Grace Farnsworth and Fabio Shakespeare. Jock has confessed everything. How Grace overheard a phone call between you, County Executive Jerome Winkle and her husband last week, about turning Garrison's Field into an industrial zone, and threatened to expose you. So you locked her up until the necessary paperwork was all taken care of, and she couldn't stop your little scheme."

Detective Kingsley had walked up to the Mayor, and now ordered him to stand, then outfitted his hands with a pair of handcuffs. Dirk wrinkled his nose, and Chase said, "Chicken dung, in case you were wondering. And you should see the other guy."

"Uncle Dirk," said Fiona. "What do you want me to do?"

Dirk sighed. "Just get me a good lawyer, honey. I'm gonna need it."

"And go back to school and get a degree," said Vesta. "Your Uncle Dirk won't be able to support you anymore."

40

*T*hings had turned a little chaotic there at the end, with Chase mud wrestling Jock, and Uncle Alec calling in reinforcements, and Grace screaming at her husband. And by the time more officers arrived on the scene, to take Jock and Gino away, and an ambulance arrived for Grace and Fabio, I guess Odelia kind of forgot about us, and so when all was said and done we were the only ones left.

Well, us and a couple of thousand chickens, of course.

So we decided to walk. It was a nice way to end the investigation. Grace and Fabio had been saved, the bad people arrested, and we could now rest on our laurels.

And we'd been walking not even a mile when we came upon an altercation. Well, altercation is perhaps a big word for the crowd that had gathered around some object.

We joined the gawking throng and when we saw what the object was, reeled back as one cat.

It was a large heap of dung, about a meter in diameter, and two meters high, and had been deposited strategically in the middle of the road.

"It's the werewolf's," one woman said.

"Yes, it has to be," said a man.

"That monster must be big!" said a third person.

"Well, did you see the pictures in the *Gazette*? That monster is huge! Big as a house!"

They all stared at the heap of werewolf doo-doo, taking pictures with their smartphones, while some members of the public had the good sense to call the police.

I could have told them the police were a little busy right now, arresting bad people, but of course they couldn't know that.

Dooley had approached the heap of dung, which was still steaming, and took a tentative sniff. "It doesn't smell like werewolf dung," he said now, rejoining us at the edge of the circle of spectators.

"It doesn't?" I asked.

I decided to put his theory to the test and approached the pile myself, taking a whiff of the penetrating odor. "Dooley is right," I said. "This isn't werewolf dung."

"And how would you know what werewolf dung smells like?" asked Brutus.

"I don't, but I know what chicken dung smells like, and this is chicken dung."

"That's it!" Dooley said. "I thought it smelled familiar."

Brutus, frowning, now decided to olfactorily sample the pile for himself, followed by Harriet. When they returned to our huddle, they both concurred that, in their professional opinion, it was indeed a big pile of chicken dung.

"Which can only mean one thing," I said.

"Oh?" said Brutus. "And what is that?"

"Someone put that pile there. Someone went to the trouble of collecting chicken dung and constructing this pile so people would think the werewolf was here."

"But why?" asked Dooley.

I shrugged. "I have no idea. But this means that maybe, just maybe, that werewolf isn't a real werewolf."

"Is it a chickenwolf, Max?" asked Dooley. "Like a mutated monster chicken?"

"I think it's not a monster but man-made."

In other words, a man in a suit. But why? And who?

It gave us something to think about while we resumed our long hike into town. And then, when we'd almost reached the finish line, Odelia's pickup suddenly showed up, driving fast in the other direction. She must have spotted us, for she immediately braked, then performed a U-turn and halted right next to us, and pushed open the door.

"I'm so sorry, guys. I forgot all about you!"

"That's all right," I said as we climbed in.

"We discovered something," Dooley said as we made ourselves comfortable on the backseat and Odelia put the car in gear.

"Me, too," she said with a smile. "Did you know that the Mayor was in cahoots with Jock and the County Executive to buy up as much land as they could, through some murky corporation, and then turn it into industrially zoned land they could sell at a much higher price?"

"That doesn't sound good," said Brutus, though clearly he hadn't understood a word she'd said, and neither had I.

But before she had a chance to explain further, Dooley blurted out, "The werewolf isn't a werewolf at all, but a human! Well, either a human or a mutated giant chicken."

"My money is on a human," I said.

Odelia thought for a moment. "And I'll bet I know who," she said, then turned that car around once more, and headed back the way we'd come!

"Hey, we just came from there!" said Harriet, who hates walking, and especially walking without a clear purpose.

"I know, but I just had an idea," said Odelia.

"Uh-oh," said Brutus, who's well familiar with Odelia's ideas. Oftentimes they will land us in trouble—or Chase knee-deep in a puddle of chicken muck.

We arrived back at the Farnsworth house, and this time she drove the car up the drive and parked in front of the house. She rang the bell, and Alicia opened the door.

"Oh, hey, Odelia," said the young woman. "Where is everybody? I just got home and there's no one here."

"Your dad is in jail," said Odelia, "your mom and Fabio are in the hospital, and I'm here to search your dad's room if I may."

Alicia blinked as she processed this information, then her face lit up. "You found my mom?"

"Yes, I did. Or actually my cats did," said Odelia. "They sniffed her out."

"And my dad is in jail?" she asked, a little more subdued.

"I'm afraid he is. He's the one who had your mother and Fabio locked up."

"But... why?"

"It's a long story, but what it all boils down to is that your father stood to gain a great deal of money by manipulating some zoning regulations. Your mother found out and had to be silenced, at least until he could carry out his plans."

Odelia stepped inside, and told us to wait on the doorstep, which we dutifully did.

Ten minutes later, she came walking out again, holding up a large suit.

And when she unfolded the suit, we saw that it was... a werewolf suit!

41

*W*e were in Marge and Tex's backyard, and Tex was manning his Webber Master-Touch super-grill again. There was nothing particularly super about his burgers, though, for even with Chase's assistance they weren't much to write home about. Tex is not a grill-meister, even though he desperately wants to be. The rest of the family copes while he practices his art. Marge, meanwhile, makes sure her family members are all well-provided for with actual edible food, and so everybody is happy. Tex, because he gets to show off his non-existent skills, and the rest of the family because they get to enjoy Marge's excellent cooking. She, contrary to her husband, is a master at her craft.

"That's love," said Dooley with a sigh.

"What is, Dooley?" I asked.

"Marge allowing her husband to believe he's a grill king."

"I guess it is," I said, as we watched Tex aim another patty into the neighbor's backyard. He'd been improving, though. He used to aim them straight into Rufus's maw, but now he also sailed a couple into Kurt's backyard, where Fifi gladly gobbled them up.

"So the werewolf doesn't exist?" asked Dooley. He still hadn't gotten over the fact that this much-vaunted beast was a figment of Jock's creativity and some careful planning.

"No, it doesn't," I said. "Jock and the Mayor and their friend who runs the county had decided they wanted to turn those old woods and those couple of shaggy farms into an industrial zone, which they could sell for a huge profit. Jock wanted to expand his farm, and that's probably how the ball got rolling. Once Mayor Dunham was elected mayor, and Jerome Winkle County Executive, they could organize this land grab through official channels. Only problem was that a couple of those farmers refused to sell, so that's where the werewolf came in. They figured that if people were scared enough, they might be encouraged to sell out. Plus, if those werewolf sightings intensified, the value of people's land would drop, making it cheaper to buy up."

"But it looked so real," said Dooley.

"Yeah, it did. Jock had the money to buy himself a top-of-the-line suit and mask."

"I knew it wasn't real," said Brutus. "I knew there was something off when I first laid eyes on that thing."

"No, you didn't," said Harriet. "You believed it was a werewolf just like the rest of us."

"And just like Victor Ball and his neighbors," I said.

"What a scheme," said Dooley. "And to think I thought the Mayor was a good mayor."

"Well, he wasn't."

"At least now Chief Alec will get to keep his job," said Brutus.

"And Abe Cornwall," Harriet added.

The Mayor and the County Executive had wanted to get rid of the Chief and the coroner when they discovered both of them had signed a petition protesting against the destruction of those woods. Rumors had started to fly about the rezoning and a petition was launched. It was enough to put Alec and Abe on the Mayor and the Executive's blacklist.

"So have you convinced Kurt to buy his dog a litter box?" asked Marge now.

"He's stubborn," said Odelia. "He says it's not natural, and he flatly refuses to get one. I told him I'd buy one for Fifi, but he says he's not a charity case and besides, it's the principle of the thing, not the money."

"You got that right," said Kurt, suddenly popping his shiny bald head over the hedge—apparently he'd snuck into Odelia's backyard simply to eavesdrop on us! "Dogs aren't meant to go on litter boxes. They're meant to be free to do their thing."

"But you have to admit, Kurt, that it is a little unhygienic," said Marge.

"I clean up after her," said Kurt stubbornly. "And that pavement sees a lot more unhygienic things than my dog's poo-poo."

"Still, she keeps using Harriet's litter box," said Marge. "And that has got to stop."

"Maybe you should teach your cats to go out in the wild, like my Fifi," said Kurt. "That way you wouldn't need a litter box, or all that expensive litter. Have you considered that you need to get rid of that litter after it's been used? You pay for the litter, and then you pay to get rid of it!"

He had a point, and Marge now acknowledged that he did.

"Look, Kurt, it's very simple," said Gran. "Either you stop that dog of yours from taking a dump in my cat's litter box, or I'm going to start taking my morning dump on your porch from now on. How does that sound?"

He shot her a nasty look, then retreated, like a turtle's head returning to its shell.

"You shouldn't talk to the neighbors like that, Ma," said Uncle Alec. "It's important we all get along."

"Oh, I get along great, it's him that's not getting along," she grunted, and pronged a piece of lettuce, then eyed it with distinct malice.

"Well, I'm sure glad we get to keep you on as chief, Chief," said Chase, clapping his superior officer on the wide back. "I was afraid you were serious about me following in your footsteps."

"I was serious!" said Uncle Alec. "I think you'd make a great chief of police."

"But you're staying on, aren't you, Alec?" asked Tex, flicking a burger patty straight into Odelia's backyard. It was sizzling hot and judging from the loud cry of anguish, it had just landed on our neighbor's bald pate. Served him right for spying on us, I guess.

"That all depends on who the next mayor is," said Alec. And when Gran's eyes started to sparkle, he immediately added, "And no, it's not gonna be me, Ma!"

"You're a mean bastard, Alec Lip," Gran snarled. "You don't even want to grant your old mother's dying wish!"

"You're not dying, Ma."

"I could be dying," she said as she stared at that piece of lettuce some more, as if it might be the final nail in her coffin.

"I'm just glad that Grace is back, and that Jock is in jail," said Marge, "where he belongs."

"Amen to that," said Tex cheerfully, unable to contain his glee to see his old love rival behind bars.

"So what's happening with Johnny and Jerry?" asked Odelia. "Any trace of those two?"

Chase shook his head sadly. "We've asked the Mexican

police to help us find them, but they've not been entirely forthcoming."

"So they're in Mexico?"

"It would appear so. At least according to the information we got from the airline."

"How much did they take?"

"According to the bank manager not that much. Maybe fifty thousand?"

"Not enough to retire on," said Uncle Alec.

"I got a nice postcard from Johnny last week," said Marge conversationally, and her words startled the entire company.

"Mom! And you didn't tell us?" Odelia cried.

"It's a very nice postcard," she said defensively. "And it was addressed to me personally, not the library."

She disappeared into the house, then returned a minute later with the card.

"'Having a nice time here on the beach in Tulum,'" Odelia read, "'but I miss the library and was wondering if you could put in a good word for me if I decide to apply for the job. Sunny greetings from Tulum, Johnny. PS: Jerry says hi.'"

"So I guess they're in Tulum," said Gran with a grin.

"Gimme that card," said Alec, and snatched it from his niece's fingers.

"Isn't that nice?" said Dooley. "Johnny wants to change careers."

"I think the only career he'll get is printing license plates," said Brutus.

"He might get a reduced sentence because he helped the authorities catch the Mayor and his cronies," I said.

And somehow I hoped that he did. Marge seemed to like Johnny, and that meant something. Marge is a librarian, and librarians are smart. They have to be, from scanning all those books.

In the meantime, I was glad this whole episode was finally

behind us. All this hawking litter and checking different types of dung had seriously worn me out, and I now longed for a nice long vacation, free from detecting or the strains of selling litter.

And just as I was about to close my eyes to take a nap, a little doggie came tripping past. It was Fifi and she gave me a wink. Harriet and the others hadn't seen her, as they'd all dozed off by then, their bellies full and their minds at ease.

Fifi tiptoed into the house through the pet flap. Moments later, she returned.

I have to say her skin looked great, and so did her fur. Even her muscularity had improved.

Could it be that cat litter was the miracle cure after all? I mean, look at us cats. Our fur is shiny, our health optimal, and our muscles nicely toned. Must be the litter, right?

And I'd just dozed off when I heard a noise and saw Rufus tiptoe past.

He disappeared into the house, then returned moments later.

I was about to take another stab at this nap thing, when a third dog came tripping up, disappeared inside, then emerged a minute later. I recognized him as Cooper the dog that had begun to favor Brutus's litter box. He had the cheek to give me a big grin and two thumbs up, before sashaying off, a swing in his step and a song on his lips.

And I'd finally fallen asleep when I was alarmed by triple screams of horror from Harriet, Brutus and Dooley. I guess the dog litter revolution rages on unabated.

Now see, that's the problem with being a cat: everybody wants to be us.

Even dogs.

Prologue

Pamela Witherspoon was walking her Pomeranian like she did every night. She took her usual route past Hampton Cove park, and watched and listened to the rare spectacle of dozens of cats all gathering in the park's playground and yowling up a storm.

Why they did this was anyone's guess. People had wondered about the strange ritual for years, and even zoologists had studied the phenomenon and been left stumped.

No one knew exactly what drove all of these cats to gather in the same spot night after night and make these strange and frankly disturbing sounds.

Dirk Benedict, world-renowned zoologist and self-declared feline specialist, had suggested that it might have something to do with this particular spot. That perhaps located in the heart of the park was an ancient burial ground where the original inhabitants of Long Island had buried their cats, and now these modern-day cats, through some ancient wisdom, came together to honor the memory of their ancestors.

Others, like Laurence Tureaud, the famous ufologist, thought this was probably the spot where aliens would one day land, when and if they finally decided on their invasion, and cats, being the mystical creatures they are, acted as the harbingers of this doom.

And then of course there were the more exotic of explanations. Some people, most notable amongst whom the renowned geologist Dwight Schultz, claimed the earth's crust was particularly thin in this exact spot, and the cats' yowls were a way of communicating with their counterparts living in the earth's core, which, still according to Mr. Schultz's more outlandish musings, wasn't solid iron and nickel, as most scientists agreed it was, but a large and complicated cave system where our counterparts live.

Pamela didn't care one hoot about all of those theories. She quite enjoyed the spectacle, and thought it was pretty. Boomer, though, didn't think it was pretty at all. On the contrary. The peppy little Pomeranian never stopped barking at the cats' meows, which from time to time earned him a shoe aimed in his direction. Usually these shoes were meant for the cats, but Boomer sometimes happened to be collateral damage.

"Pretty, isn't it, Boomer baby?" asked Pamela now.

"Woof, woof!" said Boomer in response.

"Don't you wish you were a cat in moments like these, Boomer?" asked Pamela. "So you could sing along with the rest of your lovely little friends?"

"Warrrrrf!"

Pamela smiled. Oh, how she wished sometimes she could talk to her Boomer, and understand what he said. She was pretty sure he was the smartest doggie on the planet, and every bark that rolled from his lips a nugget of wisdom.

"My own precious little genius," she said now, as she took a plastic baggie from her pocket and crouched down to clean up Boomer's doo-doo.

There had been a rumor flying around about a new rule instigated by Chief Alec that dogs would have to use a litter box from now on, but so far she hadn't heard any more.

And as she walked on, Boomer straining at the leash to get at those darn cats howling up a storm, she suddenly came upon a strange and frightening sight: a man was staggering in her direction, his arms outstretched, his fingers grasping the air!

Boomer, who'd noticed the same thing, now redirected his attention from the offending cats to the offending stranger.

And as the man reached the circle of light cast by a street-lamp, Pamela saw to her horror that his face was white as a sheet, and his skin was devastated by dozens of open sores covering its acreage. In fact it wasn't too much to say that the man looked... dead!

She uttered an involuntary little yelp of fear as the man picked up his pace and moved in her direction, his clawing hands clearly yearning to grab hold of her!

"Come on, Boomer!" said Pamela as she turned on her heel and started walking away.

The man wasn't deterred. As she glanced over her shoulder, she saw to her dismay he'd picked up his pace and was now stumbling after her, a lumbering quality to his gait.

"Run, Boomer, run!" Pamela yelled, and as she followed her own advice, they were soon running at a rapid clip, trying to escape the horrid and menacing creature.

And she'd just turned a corner when she almost bumped into a large and voluminous figure. To her not inconsiderable relief it was Chief Alec himself, Hampton Cove's stalwart chief of police.

"Chief!" she cried. "Someone is chasing me!"

"Easy now, Pamela," said the Chief in his easygoing and reassuring way. He was a man with very little hair left on top of his scalp, and a considerable paunch, and was loved by all Hampton Covians for his kindly demeanor and years of consistent selfless service.

The cop was glancing beyond her now, at the corner where any moment the stalker would appear.

"I was walking my Boomer, minding my own business, when suddenly I saw this horrible, horrible creature. And he must have seen me, too, for he immediately gave chase. Oh, Chief. Am I glad to see you!"

She'd clasped a hand to her chest, which was heaving, her heart beating a mile a minute.

"You're all right now, Pamela," rumbled the Chief. "You're perfectly safe with me."

They were both still staring at the corner, but of her assailant there was no trace.

"I swear he was right behind me, Chief," said Pamela, starting to feel a little silly now. It's one thing to be chased by a monster, but another for that monster to suddenly get cold feet the moment the constabulary arrives. She secretly wished now her assailant would show his ugly face so the Chief could see for himself she wasn't making this up.

"Let's take a look," said the Chief now. She saw that his right hand was on his weapon, and as she stayed safely behind the man's broad back, she followed as he approached the corner of the park, then cautiously glanced behind it.

"And?" she asked, her voice strained. "Is he still there?"

"Weirdest thing," grumbled the Chief.

She ventured from behind the safety of the police officer, and took a look for herself. To her surprise, the man was gone.

"Oh," she said, and even Boomer seemed surprised, for he suddenly stopped yapping.

She was growing a little hot under her collar when the Chief directed a curious look at her, the kind of look a doctor would award a patient just before calling the loony bin.

"He was there, Chief, I swear," she said.

"Oh, I believe you, Pamela. I do." But it was obvious from his demeanor that he didn't. "So can you describe this man to me?"

She nodded. "This is going to sound a little strange, Chief, but the man looked like..." She sank her teeth into her lower lip.

"Yes?" he prompted. "He looked like what?"

"Well, he looked like a—like a zombie."

Chapter One

Look, I realize that I'm one of the lucky ones. My human treats me well, my food bowl is almost always filled to the rim—except when Vena the veterinarian convinces Odelia that I have to go on a diet—and I have friends in high places. I'm referring to Dooley, who had opted to lie on top of the couch's back for some reason. I guess he likes his heights.

But some days even I experience this strange pang of unhappiness. That nebulous feeling that something is lacking and you simply can't put your paw on it.

Today was one of those days. It wasn't that my bowl was empty—when it is, I make sure to wake up my human by kneading her arm and mewling into her ear until she wakes up and rectifies her mistake. It was that what was in my bowl suddenly failed to grip.

And I blame it on that TV commercial we'd been watching for the third day in a row.

Lately my friends and I have developed the habit of watching television in the early morning, long before Odelia and Chase are up.

Odelia leaves the remote lying on the coffee table, and we'd discovered—or I should probably say Dooley has discovered, quite by accident by landing his tush on top of the remote one morning—that one click on the big red button on the remote switches on the television, and a couple of clicks will take us to one of many shopping networks, which feature, every morning between five and six, a lot of commercials for pet food.

One of those commercials had attracted our attention, and we were watching it again now, all four of us on the couch.

"The revolution in pet food continues," a very beautiful young woman dressed, for some reason, in a white lab coat, was saying, smiling a perfect toothpaste smile.

"Pet food revolution," Dooley muttered reverently, as if trying to memorize the line.

"Peppard Nutrition Revolution brings you the latest scientific research and the highest quality pet food on the market. And the best part? It's free! Sign your pet up for our free testing program and enjoy all the benefits of Peppard Pet Food free of charge."

"She said free three times," said Dooley happily. "Which must mean something."

"I guess it means the food is free," said Harriet. She was smacking her lips at the sight of a gourmet dinner being presented now on the screen. Even though the woman with the lab coat always spoke of pets and pet food, the animals on the screen were all cats.

"Lucky cats," said Brutus as he shook his head. "What do they have that we don't?"

"Access to a good manager who got them into this

commercial?" I said.

"We should be in there," said Brutus. "We should be the ones tasting that godly food."

"We could always ask Odelia to sign us up," I said. "I'm sure if she does we'd be selected."

"And why is that, Max?" asked Dooley, speaking from his high perch.

"Because Odelia is a famous reporter," I said. "And I'm sure these Peppard Pet Food people would love an article about their products in the *Gazette*, something which she could give them in exchange for our participation in this revolutionary new program."

"And I'm sure it doesn't work like that," said Harriet. "You probably have to know someone to get into the program."

"Maybe Chase could get us in?" said Dooley, obviously as eager as the rest of us to taste some of this 'revolutionary new pet food with the greatest taste and the highest-possible nutritional value on the market.'

"Chase? How would Chase be able to get us in?" scoffed Brutus.

"Chase is a cop," said Dooley, "and cops arrest people when they don't do as he says."

"I don't think Chase will arrest the Peppard people if they don't admit us into the program, Dooley," I said.

"Who is Chase going to arrest?" asked Odelia as she walked into the living room, yawning and dressed in her Betty Boop jammies and Hello Kitty slippers.

She took a seat on the couch and stared at the TV, her eyes still a little bleary. She and Chase had gone out last night on a date, and it had gotten a little late.

"We need to get into this new program," said Harriet now. "They promise its nuggets will add at least sixty percent extra shine to my coat."

"And make me lose fifty percent of my flab," I added.

"And make me seventy-five percent more butch," said Brutus.

"And make me at least forty percent more intelligent," said Dooley.

Odelia laughed. "This food can do all that? What is it? A kind of miracle cure?"

"How did you know?" asked Dooley excitedly.

On the screen, the woman in the lab coat now held up a can of that miracle food and smiled into the camera, her eyes shining with excitement, almost as if she'd tasted the food herself and loved what it had done for her. "Our scientists have developed Miracle Cure specifically with your beloved fur babies in mind. You will find that it doesn't just meet all of their needs, but makes them more healthy, strong, smart and gorgeous. Peppard Pet Food. The pet food revolution. And that's a promise, not a pitch."

"See?" said Dooley, practically vibrating with excitement. "It's a promise, not a pitch."

But Odelia didn't look convinced. "Miracle Cure? Sounds a little fishy, if you ask me."

"What's going on here?" asked Chase who'd walked into the room, barefoot and clad in a T-shirt that proclaimed he was the 'World's Greatest Pet Dad.'

"They've been watching one of those shopping networks," said Odelia, "and now they want to try this new pet food called Miracle Cure. A brand called Peppard Pet Food."

Chase stared at the screen for all of two seconds before he grunted, "Snake oil. There should probably be a law against them."

"See!" said Dooley. "Chase is going to arrest them—this is our in, you guys!"

"It's actually not available in stores yet," I said. "The only way to get the food is by entering your pets into their free testing program. Which is free," I added, hoping to convey some of my enthusiasm. "Free as in, it doesn't cost any money."

Odelia raised an eyebrow. "Don't tell me. You want to be entered into this program?"

"Yes, please!" we all shouted simultaneously.

She shook her head. "Oh, come on. It's probably just a marketing push for some new and dodgy product."

A phone number had appeared on the screen, and I now nudged Odelia's phone, which she'd left on the couch the night before.

She laughed and picked it up. "Okay, okay! I get the message." She tapped the number into her phone as Chase walked into the kitchen, shaking his head. He might be the world's greatest pet dad, but Odelia clearly was the world's greatest cat lady.

Moments later, she was talking to the Peppard Pet Food people, or at least I assumed that she was. And when she hung up and said, "It was an answering service but I left my name and number and told them I have four fur babies who can't wait to get their paws on some of those Miracle Cure nuggets," we all shared a look of utter excitement.

"You know what his means, right?" said Harriet. "We're going to be Miracle Cure pets!"

"*If* you're selected," said Odelia, dampening our excitement. "And *if* I approve of the program."

So we all crossed our digits that we would be selected, and that Odelia would approve our entry into the program.

Frankly, after having sampled every available brand of cat kibble and soft food on the market, I was dying to try something new.

Like I said, I know I'm one of the lucky ones, but even the lucky ones get bored.

Dooley had jumped down from the couch and was now tripping toward the pet door.

"Hey, where are you going?" asked Harriet.

"I'm going to ask Gran to call the same number, and also Marge," said Dooley. "It's probably like the lottery. The more tickets you buy, the bigger your chances of winning."

See what I mean? Dooley hadn't even eaten this revolutionary new cat food yet, and already it was boosting his IQ!

Chapter Two

Things were pretty slow at the doctor's office, so Vesta decided to run into the pharmacy and pick up her prescription. Even though she liked to proclaim she was as healthy as a woman half her age or less, she still was plagued with little aches and pains from time to time. Lucky for her then that her daughter had married a fine doctor, who, even though he sometimes liked to express his desire for her expedient expiration, still tried to make sure she lived as long and as happy a life as he could manage in his medical wisdom and expertise.

She walked into the pharmacy on Downing Street now and the first person she saw was Scarlett Canyon. The woman's puffy lips puffed some more, and her cat's eyes flashed even more catty than usual when she spotted her mortal enemy. She smiled.

"Oh, hi, Vesta, darling," she said in unctuous tones that reeked of insincerity. "So nice to see you."

"Scarlett," Vesta grunted unhappily. For a moment she debated turning around and walking out again, but Scarlet had seen her, and so had the half a dozen other customers waiting in line, so she forced herself to close the door behind her and proceed inside.

"So what's ailing you?" asked Scarlett. "Heart palpitations? Wonky bladder? Cancer?"

"None of the above," said Vesta, carefully hiding her

prescription behind her back. "How about you? Hemorrhoids? Flatulence? Venereal disease?"

Scarlett laughed a raucous laugh. "Oh, Vesta. You're such a hoot!"

Blanche Captor, one of the women in front of them in line, turned and said in a low voice, "Did you hear what happened to Pamela Witherspoon last night?"

Immediately all eyes turned to her. There's nothing like small-town gossip to draw people closer together. Even Vesta and Scarlett momentarily forgot their feud as they turned their attention to Blanche, a woman with cleavage as deep as her desire to gossip.

"She accosted your son last night, Vesta."

"Alec? What do you mean?" asked Vesta. She knew that her son was a real catch, being a widower with a steady job and all, but she could hardly imagine Pamela Witherspoon throwing herself in his arms. Alec might be a catch, but even though his mother, she was keenly aware her son wasn't exactly a Brad Pitt or Chris Hemsworth..

"She said she was being attacked, but when Chief Alec went to look for her attacker, he was nowhere to be found!"

"An attacker!" said Ida Baumgartner excitedly. She was one of Tex's regulars.

Blanche nodded. "By the park. Late last night."

"I heard it was a rapist," said Marcie, who was Vesta's neighbor. "And the Chief barely managed to save her. Pamela's clothes were all torn and tattered, and by the time she fell into the Chief's arms, she was only half dressed."

"A half-naked Pamela Witherspoon in the arms of a widower. Now really," said Scarlett, clucking her tongue with delight.

"Oh, baloney," said the pharmacist, a no-nonsense older gentleman answering to the improbable name of Rory Suds. "Pamela was in here first thing this morning, and she told me the whole story." All attention now focused on the pharmacist, who seemed to bask in it. "It wasn't just a man she saw. It was a zombie!"

"A zombie!" said Scarlett, clutching her not inconsiderable chest.

"Zombies don't exist, Rory," said Marcie. "Everybody knows that."

"Well, she swore up and down that that was what she saw: a real live zombie."

"That's a contradiction in terms," said Vesta. "Zombies, as a rule, are dead."

"It is possible," said Blanche, "that Pamela had been drinking. I walked past St. John's Church the other day and saw her coming out with Victor Ball." She gave her audience a meaningful look, and they all gasped in shock once more.

The whole town knew Victor Ball as a recovering alcoholic, and to be seen with him was as much as an admission of guilt—of having issues with the bottle oneself.

"Victor is sober now," said Vesta. "He told me so."

"But he's still going to Father Reilly's AA meetings," said Scarlett. "And so, apparently, is Pamela Witherspoon."

Lips were pressed together, and silent looks exchanged. It was determined therefore, and writ large in the town's lore, that Pamela Witherspoon was a raging alcoholic who had taken to accosting police chiefs in the middle of the night, half-naked and rambling on about non-existing zombies.

Rory Suds shook his grizzled head, quickly worked his way through the line of customers, and when it was finally Scarlett's turn, she cleared her voice, and said, clear as a bell, "My usual prescription for the contraceptive pill, Rory."

Vesta's head jerked up, as if stung. "Now Scarlet, really," she said. "You're not still trying to convince me you're on the pill, are you?"

"I'm not trying to convince you of anything," said Scarlett with a little laugh. "I'm on the pill, that's a fact."

"But you're my age! You passed menopause two or three decades ago!"

"Speak for yourself," said Scarlett snippily. "You may have passed your menopause but I haven't. And that's because I've been taking care of myself. As you know, I'm very sexually active, and therefore I need to protect myself from unwanted pregnancies."

"Unwanted pregnancies! You couldn't get pregnant if the Holy Ghost came down and impregnated you himself!"

Rory had returned with Scarlett's prescription and now placed it on the counter. "That'll be nineteen ninety-nine," he said, rubbing his hands with glee. He was having a good sales morning. His smile vanished when Vesta grabbed the box and stared at it.

"Um, Vesta, you can't just grab someone else's medication," he pointed out.

"Yes, Vesta," said Scarlett with a smile. "That's just plain rude."

But Vesta was studying the pillbox closely. "This is impossible," she said. "Rory, you don't believe this nonsense, do you? A woman of seventy-five can't possibly still be on the pill, right?"

Rory tilted his head. "I'm afraid I'm not at liberty to discuss Mrs. Canyon's particular…"

"*Miss* Canyon," said Scarlett. "I never married, which is probably why I'm something of a medical anomaly. Isn't that what you told me just the other day, Rory, darling?"

Rory gave a curt and embarrassed little laugh. "It's really not my place to—"

"Yes or no, Rory," Vesta demanded. "Has she passed menopause or not?"

But the pharmacist merely tapped the prescription and

shrugged. "Like I was trying to point out, it's not a pharmacist's place to make these kinds of judgments. If Scarlett's doctor prescribed her the contraceptive pill, he must have done so for a good reason."

Vesta now picked up the prescription. It was as she had surmised: written up by Tex. She frowned darkly. "I don't know what game you're playing, Scarlett, but I can promise you this: I'll get to the bottom of your so-called medical miracle and I'll do it right now!"

And as she stalked off, Rory called after her, "Vesta! Did you need something?"

But she was already slamming the door. Scarlett might have fooled Tex, but she wasn't fooling her. No way a seventy-five-year-old woman could still be in danger of getting pregnant. And she was going to prove it, too.

Chapter Three

Chase Kingsley breezed into the police precinct and was greeted by Dolores, who waved him over the moment he walked through the door.

"Pssst!" said the grumpy-faced and heavily-made-up desk sergeant. She glanced around, as if expecting spies to pop out of the woodwork and listen in on their conversation.

"What is it this time?" asked Chase, who knew Dolores well enough to know she was eager to spill some gossip.

"It's the big boss!" she said.

"The Chief? What about him?"

"Listen to this. Do you know Pamela Witherspoon? No, well, good for you. She's a widow," she said, making it sound as if Pamela was some kind of monster. "And last night she jumped the Chief in the park! Buck naked, she was, and dragging him into the bushes, asking him to make sweet, sweet love to her right then and there, if you please!"

"Huh," said Chase. "And? Did he comply?"

"Of course he didn't comply, you idiot! He told her he was on duty, and as everyone knows, cops on duty can't just engage in any frivolous activity they damn well please. So he plucked her naked bosoms from his chest and told her to put some clothes on. And listen to this—he then escorted her home, like the sap—I mean gentleman that he is."

"Right," said Chase, too skeptical for Dolores's taste, though, for she frowned.

"You don't believe me? Ask the Chief. He'll tell you it's the God's honest truth. The only part of the story I'm still a bit fuzzy on is what happened after he walked her home. I heard she invited him in for a quickie, but my sources weren't clear on whether he was able to restrain himself and walk away, or if he went in and enjoyed a midnight nookie in the widow's lair. Ask him, will you?" she added, as she picked up the phone. "And then tell me." And as Chase walked away, she yelled after him, "Don't forget to ask him, Chase!"

He held up a hand and set foot for the coffee machine. He had no intention of asking the Chief anything, but had to admit his curiosity was piqued. No smoke without fire, was one of Dolores's favorite expressions, and he had to admit that more often than not there was some truth to it.

And as the Chief joined him and held out his cup for a refill, Chase eyed him with a keen expression on his face. "You look like you haven't slept a wink last night, Chief."

"Oh, don't you start, too," the Chief grumbled. "You'll never believe what happened to me. Zombies!"

"Zombies? I thought it was widows that had kept you up all night."

The Chief rolled his eyes. "Dolores!"

"Yeah, if she's to be believed you've been up all night doing the horizontal mambo with Pamela Witherspoon."

"What?!"

Chase grinned. "You old dog, you."

"Listen," said the Chief, tapping Chase on the chest with a disconcerted finger. "I never touched the woman, all right? I was getting some fresh air when I bumped into her. She claimed she saw a zombie, but try as I might I was unable to locate said zombie, but I could tell she'd had a big scare, so I walked her and her dog Boomer home, and that's as far as it went. I never set foot inside her house, no matter what anyone says."

"They also claim she jumped you, buck naked, and dragged you into the bushes for some sweet nookie."

"Oh, God!" the Chief said. "Sometimes I hate this town, Chase. I really do."

"So zombies, huh?"

"That's what she said. A man with a face full of sores, white as a sheet, eyes wide and scary, dressed in dirty clothes. As she described him he'd just crawled out of the grave and was now walking the streets, looking for fresh victims to feed on. He chased her around the park until she bumped into me. At which point he mysteriously vanished."

"She hadn't been drinking by any chance?"

"No, as far as I could tell she was stone-cold sober. Besides, I know Pamela. She doesn't drink." He scratched his few remaining hairs. "It's baffling, Chase. Baffling."

"Well, I'm sure it was just a bum who scared the bejesus out of your Pamela."

"She's not my Pamela!" the Chief insisted, gritting his teeth.

"Whatever you say, Chief," said Chase, clapping the other man on the back.

"Please tell Dolores not to keep spreading these tall tales. I know she listens to you."

"I'll tell her. Not sure what good it'll do, but I'll tell her," he assured the older man.

And as the Chief returned to his office, shaking his head and muttering strange oaths under his breath, Chase took a sip from his coffee and promptly spat it out again.

ABOUT NIC

Nic Saint is the pen name for writing couple Nick and Nicole Saint. They've penned novels in the romance, cat sleuth, middle grade, suspense, comedy and cozy mystery genres. Nicole has a background in accounting and Nick in political science and before being struck by the writing bug the Saints worked odd jobs around the world (including massage therapist in Mexico, gardener in Italy, restaurant manager in India, and Berlitz teacher in Belgium).

When they're not writing they enjoy Christmas-themed Hallmark movies (whether it's Christmas or not), all manner of pastry, comic books, a daily dose of yoga (to limber up those limbs), and spoiling their big red tomcat Tommy.

www.nicsaint.com

The Mysteries of Max

Purrfect Murder

Purrfectly Deadly

Purrfect Revenge

Purrfect Heat

Purrfect Crime

Purrfect Rivalry

Purrfect Peril

Purrfect Secret

Purrfect Alibi

Purrfect Obsession

Purrfect Betrayal

Purrfectly Clueless

Purrfectly Royal

Purrfect Cut

Purrfect Trap

Purrfectly Hidden

Purrfect Kill

Purrfect Boy Toy

Purrfectly Dogged

Purrfectly Dead

Box Set 1 (Books 1-3)

Box Set 2 (Books 4-6)

Box Set 3 (Books 7-9)

Box Set 4 (Books 10-12)

Box Set 5 (Books 13-15)

Box Set 6 (Books 16-18)

Purrfect Santa

Purrfectly Flealess

Nora Steel

Murder Retreat

The Kellys

Murder Motel

Death in Suburbia

Emily Stone

Murder at the Art Class

Washington & Jefferson

First Shot

Alice Whitehouse

Spooky Times

Spooky Trills

Spooky End

Spooky Spells

Ghosts of London

Between a Ghost and a Spooky Place

Public Ghost Number One

Ghost Save the Queen

Box Set 1 (Books 1-3)

A Tale of Two Harrys

Ghost of Girlband Past

Ghostlier Things

Charleneland

Deadly Ride

Final Ride

Neighborhood Witch Committee

Witchy Start

Witchy Worries

Witchy Wishes

Saffron Diffley

Crime and Retribution

Vice and Verdict

Felonies and Penalties (Saffron Diffley Short 1)

The B-Team

Once Upon a Spy

Tate-à-Tate

Enemy of the Tates

Ghosts vs. Spies

The Ghost Who Came in from the Cold

Witchy Fingers

Witchy Trouble

Witchy Hexations

Witchy Possessions

Witchy Riches

Box Set 1 (Books 1-4)

The Mysteries of Bell & Whitehouse

One Spoonful of Trouble

Two Scoops of Murder

Three Shots of Disaster

Box Set 1 (Books 1-3)

A Twist of Wraith

A Touch of Ghost

A Clash of Spooks

Box Set 2 (Books 4-6)

The Stuffing of Nightmares

A Breath of Dead Air

An Act of Hodd

Box Set 3 (Books 7-9)

A Game of Dons

Standalone Novels

When in Bruges

The Whiskered Spy

ThrillFix

Homejacking

The Eighth Billionaire

The Wrong Woman

Printed in Great Britain
by Amazon